WILLIAM

SHAKESPEARE'S

GET THEE BACK

TO THE FUTURE!

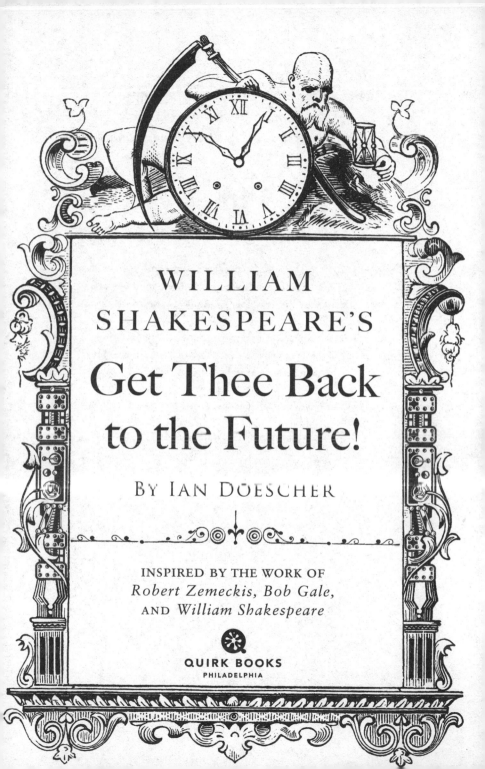

WILLIAM SHAKESPEARE'S
Get Thee Back to the Future!

BY IAN DOESCHER

INSPIRED BY THE WORK OF
Robert Zemeckis, Bob Gale,
AND *William Shakespeare*

QUIRK BOOKS
PHILADELPHIA

To Josh, Chris, Nathan, Travis, Ben, and Pete—
And all the other friends from Alameda—
Whom I first met in 1985
And still am proud to call my friends today

A Pop Shakespeare Book

Library of Congress Cataloging in Publication Number: 2018943043

ISBN: 978-1-68369-094-8

Printed in Canada

Typeset in Sabon

Designed by Doogie Horner
Text by Ian Doescher
Interior illustrations by Kent Barton
Cover illustration by Hugh Fleming
Production management by John J. McGurk

Quirk Books
215 Church Street
Philadelphia, PA 19106
quirkbooks.com

10 9 8 7 6 5 4 3 2 1

THE WILLIAM SHAKESPEARE'S
STAR WARS SERIES

The Phantom of Menace: Star Wars Part the First
The Clone Army Attacketh: Star Wars Part the Second
Tragedy of the Sith's Revenge: Star Wars Part the Third
Star Wars: Verily, A New Hope
The Empire Striketh Back: Star Wars Part the Fifth
The Jedi Doth Return: Star Wars Part the Sixth
The Force Doth Awaken: Star Wars Part the Seventh
Jedi the Last: Star Wars Part the Eighth

THE POP SHAKESPEARE SERIES
Much Ado About Mean Girls

A NOTE ABOUT
THE SERIES

Welcome to the world of Pop Shakespeare!

Each book in this series gives a Shakespearean makeover to your favorite movie or television show, re-creating each moment from the original as if the Bard of Avon had written it himself. The lines are composed in iambic pentameter, and the whole is structured into acts and scenes, complete with numbered lines and stage directions.

Astute readers will be delighted to discover Easter eggs, historical references, and sly allusions to Shakespeare's most famous plays, characters, and themes, which you can learn more about in the author's Afterword. A Reader's Guide is also included, for those who want to learn more about Shakespeare's style.

LIST OF ILLUSTRATIONS

Frontispiece   PAGE 5

"Now shall I grasp the back end of this car—
A horseless carriage fashion'd out of steel
And power'd by the strength of fuel and flame."   PAGE 21

"Pay heed: preserve the tower of the clock!
Our grand clock tower needeth your swift aid!"   PAGE 29

"Unless mine eyes deceive, before me is
The most distinctive silver frame of the
DeLorean—a car most nonpareil."   PAGE 40

"My loyal Einstein hath, e'en here, become
The first time traveler the world hath known."   PAGE 46

"Alas! We two are in a quagmire now.
They strike at us with murderous intent."   PAGE 56

"Art thou call'd Calvin Klein?
For on thine underwear it is display'd."   PAGE 79

"The flux capacitor—I know it well.
Behold, my friend, the work of thirty years . . . "   PAGE 88

"Great Scott! I prithee, let me see again
The photograph of thou and siblings too."   PAGE 94

"O Marty, be thy wheels not square, but round,
Else thou shalt nowhere go."   PAGE 130

"Hands, precious hands, play on these mellow strings,
Support the song that joins these two as one . . . "   PAGE 141

"The sign says Lone Pine Mall, not Twin Pine, strange—
Have all my memories chang'd?"   PAGE 155

"Behold, big Biff, who waxeth presently."   PAGE 161

WILLIAM SHAKESPEARE'S
GET THEE BACK TO THE FUTURE!

DRAMATIS PERSONAE

CHORUS

MARTY MCFLY, *a boy of the future*

JENNIFER PARKER, *Marty's paramour*

DOCTOR EMMETT "DOC" BROWN, *his mentor*

EINSTEIN, *Doc's canine companion*

GEORGE MCFLY, *Marty's father*

LORRAINE BAINES MCFLY, *Marty's mother*

DAVE *and* LINDA MCFLY, *Marty's siblings*

BIFF TANNEN, *a brute*

SKINHEAD, 3-D, *and* MATCH, *Biff's thugs*

SAM *and* STELLA BAINES, *Lorraine's parents*

MILTON, SALLY, TOBY, *and* JOEY BAINES, *Lorraine's siblings*

SIR STRICKLAND, *school headmaster*

GOLDIE WILSON, *a politician*

MA *and* PA PEABODY, *farmers*

SHERMAN *and* SIS PEABODY, *their children*

MARVIN BERRY AND THE STARLIGHTERS, *merry music makers*

VARIOUS RESIDENTS OF HILL VALLEY

LIBYANS

PROLOGUE

Hill Valley, California, in the New World.

Enter CHORUS.

CHORUS   Now, gentles, pray your patience for this play.
            In heart and mind, let fancy hold its sway—
            Ne'er has there been such whimsy on the stage,
            E'en when Andronicus was all the rage.
            To wit: we shall transport ye these two hours,   5
            Enablèd by our keen dramatic pow'rs.
            Ere ye depart, we'll proffer such surprise,
            Not one of ye, my friends, shall trust your eyes.
            Eyes—yea, and ears—attend unto our tale,
            In which we'll carry ye beyond the pale.   10
            Go with us, prithee, past your common sense,
            Herein we'll voyage years four hundred hence.
            Time travel! Such is our agenda bold—
            Yea, from our author's mind shall this unfold.
            For this endeavor, England we must leave,   15
            In far America our tale we weave.
            View wonders! On our stage do we arrive—
            E'en late October, nineteen eighty-five.

                                             [Exit.

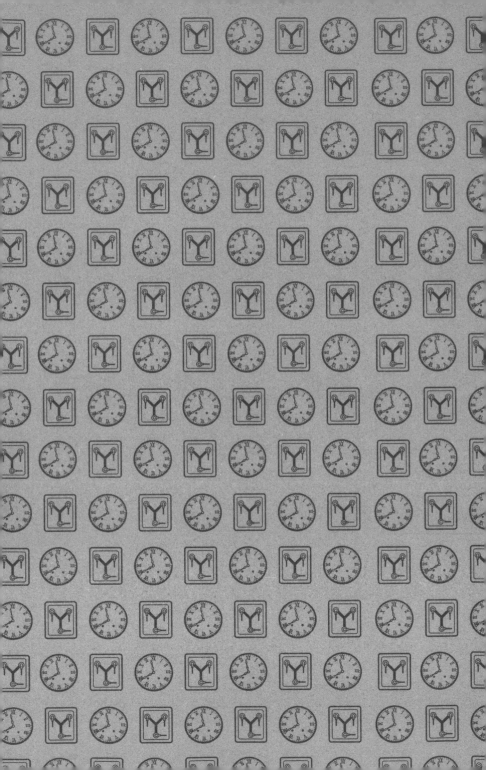

ACT I

SCENE 1

The year 1985. At Doc Brown's house.

Enter MARTY McFLY.

MARTY   Let fame, that all hunt after in their lives,
Live register'd upon my brazen tomb
And then grace me in the disgrace of death;
When, spite of cormorant devouring time,
Th'endeavor of this present breath may buy   5
That honor which shall bate his scythe's keen edge
And make me heir of all eternity.
Yet though I speak of death-defeating fame,
A simpler fate befits my humble state.
A lad of seventeen, my fondest hopes   10
Soar far beyond the custom of my years,
Which still do fall three fewer than a score.
Whilst all my friends waste time in vain pursuits,
I long for something higher than the rest.
Perhaps this longing, though, is but a symbol   15
Of that poor life that I do daily lead.
My parents poor, my siblings' prospects weak,
Our days in the Estates of Lyon just
A hollow tapestry of human life.
Beneath this melancholy promise, though,   20
I see a vision of a better day,
The sight of which doth flow from double source:
First, mine own paramour, my Jennifer,
The ever-fav'rite object of my heart.

And second, my dear friend in awe and wonder—   25
E'en Doctor Emmett Brown, whom I call Doc.
His house is like another home to me,
With less of strife and quarrels than mine own.
A place of mental curiosity,
Where to experiment is all the aim.   30
Doc is a scientist of brilliant mind,
Inventing new contraptions ev'ry day.
Although the man doth have a genius brain,
His eccentricities have kept him from
The public recognition he deserveth.   35
As I make entrance to Doc's busy home,
I find there's neither man nor beast herein.
Doc's many gadgets and creations, though,
Surround me as if I were lost at sea
And ev'ry apparatus were the water.   40
Behold these clocks which run in perfect time,
A hundred such devices—yea, or more—
Of varied style and movement, gear and spring,
Each tick the perfect echo of the rest,
Each tock in step, as to a drummer's beat.   45
A radio begins to sound, and brings
A stranger's voice unbidden to the room.
Then doth a timer ring, and on the instant
The smell of brewing coffee strikes the air,
Once programm'd for the time by Doc's own hand.   50
A television—wondrous miracle—
Turns on by force of automated lever,
Whereon a telecaster doth announce
The recent theft of some plutonium.
A charcoal slab of that, which once was bread,   55

Emerges from a toasting silver box.
Another gizmo starts with buzzing sound,
Then opens food for Einstein, Doc's pet dog,
Whose shaggy, graying hair is partner to
That which doth grow atop of Doc's own pate.   60
The bowl o'erflows—hath Einstein not been here?
Besides these few inventions, other bits
Of knick and knack are posted on the walls—
A tale torn from a newspaper of old,
Which tells the story of the mansion Brown,   65
Which, sometime more than twenty years ago,
Did burn with mighty pyre and restless flame.
This tragedy I never have discuss'd
With Doc, since he and I did friends become.
The portraits, too, of various inventors   70
Adorn the walls, as if to watch Doc work
And bring their inspiration to his toil.
Ne'er have I seen Doc's house in such a state
Of disarray, and yet I do confess:
These curiosities and implements   75
Form but a backdrop to my soul's desire,
The reason I have hither come this morn:
To play my lute upon Doc's system vast,
Which he hath gladly giv'n me leave to do.
I turn the dials and switches to the height,   80
To maximize the power of the sound.
These small controls shall amplify my lute
An 'twere a thousand lutes did play at once.
The overdrive is set to th'hundred mark,
And all the levels rise unto the brink.   85
My lute I do connect unto the board,

Prepar'd with single pluck of sheep-gut string
Here to unleash a beast of rock and roll.

> [*Marty plays and is blown back*
> *by the sound of the speaker, which*
> *then explodes. The phone rings.*

Enter DOCTOR EMMETT BROWN, *talking on phone,*
and EINSTEIN, *both above on balcony.*

DOC	Hail, Marty, art thou there?
MARTY	—Good Doc, forsooth!

Where art thou, friend? For I came to thy house   90
Expecting I should find thee at thy breakfast.

DOC   Ah! Deo gratias that thou art found—
And, also, that thou art both safe and whole.
Canst thou meet me tonight, at Twin Pines Mall,
Upon the very strike of one fifteen?   95
A major breakthrough I have made, my friend,
And shall thy brave assistance then require.

MARTY   Thou wouldst engage me thither, at the hour
Of one fifteen, which after midnight comes?
When normal folk do lie abed and sleep,   100
We two shall be outside, adventuring?

DOC   We shall, and thou shalt ne'er forget the night.

MARTY   What is the matter that doth move thee so?
And say, where hast thou been the livelong week,
Whilst for thee I have search'd with urgency?   105

DOC   Engag'd in testing mine experiments.

MARTY   Pray, what of Einstein? Is the pup with thee?

DOC   Indeed, he sitteth at my feet e'en now.

MARTY   Thy house, it is in shambles—didst thou know?

All thine equipment thou didst leave to run,   110
Some six or seven days now, by my troth.

DOC   Equipment, sayest thou? The very word
            Doth prompt remembrance of another thing:
            The amplifier for thy lute thou shouldst
            Not use at present, for there is a chance—   115
            Be it but slight indeed, still there's a chance—
            The system may o'erload and blast the whole.

MARTY   Thus shall I keep in mind. [*Aside:*] Had he but been
            Five minutes sooner, this advice would help.

DOC   'Tis well. I shall, then, see thy face tonight—   120
            I bid thee, Marty, to forget it not:
            A quarter past the stroke of one o'clock,
            At Twin Pines Mall. I'll see thee soon.

MARTY   —Indeed.
                              [*All the clocks begin chiming.*
            Alas, what ringing! Why hath this commenc'd,
            The tintinnabulations of the bells?   125

DOC   Peace! Count the clock.

MARTY   —The clock hath stricken eight.

DOC   A-ha! Then mine experiment hath work'd!
            They run as slowly as a tortoise gait,
            Behind by minutes counting twenty-five!

MARTY   What shocking words are these thou speak'st to me?   130
            What presage of mine own delay'd arrival?
            What prelude to a future punishment?
            What fable of a race against the clock?
            Is't true, what thou dost calmly say to me?
            The time is verily eight twenty-five?   135

DOC   Precisely—science is not lost on thee!

MARTY   O, fie upon it! I must play the hare,

And skip most jauntily upon my path,
For I am caught up late for school—again.

DOC   Godspeed, then, Marty, on thy merry way!   140

            [*Exeunt Doc and Einstein from balcony.*
                         Marty leaves Doc's house.

Enter various RESIDENTS OF HILL VALLEY *upon the streets.*

MARTY   I leave anon, my vehicle withal—
A piece of wood with wheels numb'ring four
On which I stand, whilst pushing with one foot.
This skateboard must convey me hence apace,

That I may swiftly to the schoolhouse fly.   145
Now shall I grasp the back end of this car—
A horseless carriage fashion'd out of steel
And power'd by the strength of fuel and flame.
The ride takes me past many jovial
Hill Valley residents and citizens,   150
Who wave at me, a youth of their acquaintance.
The driver of the car hath notic'd me
As I do use his speed to make my way.
A withering and friendless look he gives,
Belike unhappy with his hanger-on—   155
The new caboose for which he did not ask,
The barnacle that fastens to his rock.
We pass the signs for Baron Goldie Wilson,
The noble leader of our humble town.
He seeks another term of office soon   160
Beneath the banner of his motto proud,
E'en "Hon'sty, Decency, Integrity."
          [*Exeunt citizens as Marty approaches school.*
Hill Valley High School: I am here at last,
And hopefully shall not be punishèd
For my belated ingress to the school.   165

          Enter JENNIFER PARKER.

                  My love, heart of my heart, my Jennifer!
JENNIFER   Thou comest late again, sweet Marty, and
           If thou wouldst 'scape the ire of our headmaster—
           Sir Strickland, who doth fiercely search for thee—
           Go not that way, but follow on with me.   170
           If thou art caught, thou shalt be written down

              As being tardy four times in a row.

              This hallway mayhap shall give passage safe.

MARTY   This time 'twas not my fault, for I did fall

              Beneath the whimsy of Doc's genius mind,   175

              Which ever hath a new scheme, and which did—

              For trial of what theory I know not—

              Set ev'ry clock within his house behind.

Enter SIR STRICKLAND.

STRICK.   The utt'rance of that name, the name of Doc,

              Falls on mine ear an 'twere a pestilence   180

              That shall set fire unto my brain at once.

              Am I to understand that thou, McFly,

              May still be found within the company

              Of Doctor Emmett Brown, that hapless man?

              Now to your punishments, ye naughty scamps: 185

              Miss Parker, thou hast earn'd a tardy slip,

              The twin of which I give to thee, McFly,

              Which totals four upon successive days.

              Young man, to thee I'll proffer some advice,

              A ducat's worth, yet nobly, freely giv'n: 190

              The man thou callest Doc, this Doctor Brown—

              Though doctor of what science I know not,

              Nor whereby he hath earn'd the title, nay—

              He is a danger to himself and thee,

              A senseless madman and a lunatic.   195

              If thou with him dost spend thy wasted days,

              It shall be only trouble that thou find'st.

MARTY   Forsooth, your words have quite convinc'd me, sir.

STRICK.   Thy problem is thine attitude, McFly,

          Which goeth e'er before thee like a flag,   200
          Wav'd high—a standard with no standards, yea—
          Announcing unto all, "Here comes a slacker,
          A worthless imp, a lazy, wayward fool."
          How thou dost of thy father make me think,
          Who was a slacker for the record books.   205

MARTY   These words I'll take with me, if I may go.

STRICK.   I could not help but notice that thy band—
          The merry minstrels thou dost play withal—
          Shall make audition in the afternoon
          So that you may perform at our school dance.   210
          Yet wherefore even make attempt, McFly?
          There is but little chance thou shalt succeed;
          Thine apple falls too near thy father's tree.
          Ne'er did a person by the name McFly
          Amount to anything or make a mark   215
          On all our proud Hill Valley history.

MARTY   Yet history shall change soon, you shall see.

                          [Exeunt.

SCENE 2

The school auditorium.

Enter several DANCE COMMITTEE MEMBERS.

COMM. 1   In working for a living, I do strive
          To put my heart and soul in ev'ry task.

Today, within this perfect world of ours,
My task, stuck with you, friends, is no more hard
Than to ascend the rung of Jacob's ladder,   5
As if our group were angels, back in time.
The youth of our age, cruising to new heights,
Did hear our music's shape, said, "That's not me,
I want a new drug for my youthful ears."
They say, "If this is it, we want it not."   10
Their hearts dislik'd the circles of our songs,
Thus they decided 'tis hip to be square.
They fin'lly found a home in their new sound—
They think it is some kind of wonderful.
It hit me like a hammer when I heard it,   15
For bad is bad when it doth strike mine ears.
I know what I like, friends, and verily
'Tis not their music, nay. Yet, it's all right—
Don't fight it, so say I. Accept their music,
Give me the keys and beats and instruments!   20
Do you believe in love? So do our youth,
And thus, the heart of rock and roll we'll hear,
This music that the pow'r of love releaseth.

Enter MARTY MCFLY *with his band,* THE PINHEADS.
Enter JENNIFER PARKER *aside, watching.*

MARTY   Our very best we'll play for you today,
     That you may deem us worthy to join in   25
     Hill Valley High's own battle of the bands.
     We call ourselves the Pinheads—now, boys, play!

PINHEADS   [*singing:*] Bet not thy future days upon
         One rolling of the dice,

Yet think of lightning, here then gone—   30
 It never striketh twice.
If thou art wise, then hear my song,
 And listen to my rhyme,
To save the future from great wrong,
 O, get thee back in time.   35

COMM. 1 I prithee, cease at once this noisome noise,
Whilst I give ye the news of our resolve:
Thou art too loud to earn a place this year.
We'll hear the next group at another time,
When that our ears have made recovery.   40

 [Exeunt committee members and the Pinheads.
 Jennifer and Marty walk outside.

Enter various RESIDENTS OF HILL VALLEY.
A car passes by with Goldie Wilson's image upon it, and an
advertisement can be heard playing on the RADIO.

RADIO [*in car:*] Elect again our Baron Goldie Wilson,
For truly, progress is his middle name.

MARTY "Too loud," these are the words with which they greet
A music for a newfound age and time?
I'd not believe my senses, were I not   45
Rejected to my face two minutes back.
When shall I ever have a chance to play
Before an audience with will to hear?

JENNIFER Yet one rejection endeth not the world,
Nor doth it close the door on all thy dreams.   50

MARTY Belike musician shall not be my trade,
For with an audience I strike no chords.

JENNIFER And yet thy talent sings in ev'ry note.

The record thou hast made of thy sweet songs,
With which thou wilt audition once again,   55
Doth move me with its splendid melodies.
Send it, I bid thee, to a music shoppe
That will appreciate thine aptitude.
As Doc doth often say—

MARTY   —Forsooth, I know:
"When thou dost put thy mind unto the task,   60
Thou mayst accomplish nearly anything."

                              [Two women walk by and Marty
                                   watches them pass.

JENNIFER   Turn not thine eyes, but love the one thou'rt with.
             Doc Brown's advice is worthy of thine ear.

MARTY   Think on this possibility, my joy:
             What if I send this record unto them,   65
             They listen to the tunes and like them not,
             Do thereupon reject me and my songs,
             And tell me that I simply have no gift?
             In doing so, they would disrupt my future
             Rejection thus would be unbearable.   70
             Alas, how I do sound like mine old man—
             My father, who doth often grumble so.

JENNIFER   The man is not as bad as thou dost say.
             Remember, he shall let us have his car
             Tomorrow, wherewith we shall flee the town,   75
             Our school, our families, and ev'ryone.

MARTY   Behold, across the avenue—dost see?
             A truck of such great beauty, grace, and pow'r,
             Bedeck'd in shades of blackest, darkest night,
             A thing of splendor, hotter than the sun.   80
             Someday, one such as this will be our own:

	Imagine, thou and I ride to the lake,	
	Put bags for sleeping in the rear compartment,	
	Lie underneath the firmament, alone.	
JENNIFER	Cease, love, for to imagine brings but pain	85
	When it may never be. Pray, tell me, dost	
	Thy mother know about tomorrow night?	
MARTY	Nay, never, for the lady would erupt.	
	She thinketh I am bound away with friends	
	Upon a camping venture and no more.	90
	If she did know I plann'd to go with thee,	
	Her ire would rise unto the boiling point.	
	She would give me a mountain built of words	
	About her own behavior as a child,	
	How she did never try her parent's will	95
	Or play the queen within a game of hearts.	
	Methinks she was conceiv'd within a convent	
	And born unto a family of nuns.	
JENNIFER	She would keep thee respectable, I'll warrant.	
MARTY	She faileth at the task.	
JENNIFER	—Yea, happily.	100

They begin to embrace. Enter a CLOCK TOWER BOOSTER.

BOOSTER	Pay heed: preserve the tower of the clock!	
	Our grand clock tower needeth your swift aid!	
	Our noble Baron Wilson hath a plan,	
	Which shall repair our weary, broken clock!	
	'Twas thirty years ago the clock was struck	105
	By lightning from the heav'nly clouds above,	
	As if it did delight e'en Zeus himself	
	To stop the clock with bolt and marksman's aim,	

Destroying, then, the clock that irk'd him so.
It hath not told the time aright since then.   110
And we—the keen Hill Valley Preservation
Society—shall keep it as 'twas destin'd.
We, swift as shadow, short as any dream,
Brief as the lightning in the collied night,
Collect as many alms as ye can give   115
So to preserve the clock just as it is,
Maintain our history and heritage!

MARTY   Here is a coin for all thy labors, madam.
            [*Aside:*] Yea, also shall it get thee quickly gone,
            No more our loving moment t'interrupt.   120

BOOSTER   My greatest thanks, good lad, for thy support.
            Take thou this pamphlet, which shall tell thee more
            Of how thou mayst join in our effort just.

MARTY   Go now, I bid thee—with thee goes my hopes.
                              [Exeunt booster and other residents.
               [To Jennifer:] Sweet, where were we before we were
                                             disturb'd? 125
JENNIFER   Upon the prelude to a tender kiss.

               They begin to embrace. Enter JENNIFER'S FATHER.

FATHER   Say Jennifer, the time hath come to go.
JENNIFER   The time is never perfect, is it, love?
               My father comes, and I must go with him.
MARTY   Tonight I'll call on thee.
JENNIFER   —This evening I'll   130
               Be found at my grandmother's house. Her number
               I'll write for thee upon this pamphlet white.
MARTY   *[aside:]* This must be something more than mere desire,
               When but to watch her write with pen and ink
               Doth stir my heart to gentle, loving thoughts.   135
JENNIFER   For now, farewell, until another time.
                       [She kisses him. Exeunt Jennifer and her father.
MARTY   I read the words she penn'd upon the page—
               "I love thee," she hath written. O, my sweet!
               Such unexpected joy, such wondrous glee
               Inspires a sonnet, form'd in melody: 140
               [Sings:] The pow'r of love, O 'tis a curious thing:
               It changeth hawks into a gentle dove,
               It maketh one man weep, another sing,
               More than a feeling: 'tis the pow'r of love.
               'Tis tougher e'en than diamonds, rich like cream,   145
               It makes a bad one good, a wrong one right,
               'Tis stronger, harder than a wench's dream,

The pow'r of love shall keep thee home at night.
When first thou feelest it, may make thee sad,
When next thou feelest it, may be profound,   150
Yet when thou learnest this, thou shalt be glad:
It is this power makes the world go 'round.
'Tis strong and sudden, sent by heav'n above,
It may just save thy life, this pow'r of love.

> [*Exit.*

SCENE 3

At the McFly house.

Enter BIFF TANNEN.

BIFF A thousand sculptors, given time enow,
    Of ev'ry aptitude and skill possess'd,
    Resounding though their fame and plaudits be,
    Though they had perfect tools and finest stone—
    Could ne'er produce so great a form as mine.   5
    For I am Biff, the paragon of men—
    Who destin'd was for greatness, by my troth.

Enter MARTY MCFLY *and* GEORGE MCFLY.

MARTY Alack, what horrid scene is this I find?
    Our fam'ly car outside—a heap, a wreck,
    Deliver'd unto its too-sudden grave   10

By gloomy truck that like the reaper comes
And hither brings the shell of all my hopes—
My freedom dead, come to a crashing halt.

BIFF   [*to George:*] How couldst thou lend me, who hast
                                      giv'n thee much,
    A car that hath a blind spot near the side?   15

GEORGE   A blind spot, eh? Such did I never witness.

BIFF   Belike I should be dead, may have been kill'd!

GEORGE   No blind spot spotted I when I go driving.
    [*To Marty:*] Good even, son, and welcome home this
                                    evening.

BIFF   Mayhap 'tis thou, McFly, and not thy car,   20
    Which art the blind one. Call'st thou me a knave?
    How canst thou reconcile the wreck outside
    With thy denial of the car's blind spot?

GEORGE   Good Biff, thou art an honorable person—
    So are we all, all honorable people.   25
    May I assume that thou shalt pay the charges
    To fix the car that thou hast lately ruin'd?
    Canst thou give me assurance of insurance?

BIFF   Insurance, ha! The car is thine, McFly.
    Seek thou no reassurance from my lips,   30
    For no insurance I maintain shall e'er
    Pay for thy car—but thine insurance, thine!
    I prithee, mine endurance do not test.
    Whilst we do speak of payment, what of this?—
    My doublet is awash in sticky beer,   35
    Which I, perforce, did spill when I was struck.
    Who shall pay for the cleaning of my coat?
    Moreover, hast thou finish'd my reports?

GEORGE   In truth, they are not yet completed, sirrah.

Because they are not due until far later—   40
      [Biff grabs George and begins knocking on his
            head with his knuckles.

BIFF   Shall I have cause to bash thee on thy pate?
Is any brain herein, that I must knock
To find out whether there is one at home?
Use thou thy mind and not thy voice, McFly—
I must have time enow to write their words   45
In mine own hand, as if the work were mine.
Hast thou the consequence consider'd, George,
Should I submit some work first penn'd by thee,
Writ in the style and manner of thy hand?
I would, most instantly, be told "You're fired!"—   50
Words I would rather say myself than hear.
Thou wouldst not want that fate for Biff, wouldst thou?

GEORGE   *[aside:]* In truth, there's naught could make more elated.
Yet such a thought I'll keep to mine own counsel—
To speak this sentiment could prove most deadly.   55

BIFF   Wouldst thou? Speak now, I would hear thy reply.

GEORGE   Of course not, Biff, 'twould be a true disaster.
Tonight, I shall complete the needed statements,
Deliv'ring them to thee upon the morrow.
Shall this suffice?

BIFF   —It shall, yet not too soon—   60
My wont 'tis to sleep late on Saturday.
Behold below, McFly, thy shoe's untied.
      [George looks and Biff knocks him on the chin.
Thou art predictable as time itself,
Which ever runneth forward, never back,
And counteth off the seconds of our life.   65
Thou art too gullible by half, McFly,

As one who would believe a jester's trick.
Meanwhile, thy cottage doth not disappoint,
Except for thy most meagre choice of ale.
I hither tow thy car, unto thy house—   70
Is such cheap swill the best thou canst provide?

MARTY   [*aside*:] Look on this man, a villain in the height,
And fouler than a vulture at a corpse.

BIFF   [*to Marty*:] Upon what lookest thou, thou arse-like
                                                pate?

When thou dost see thy mother, wish her well—   75
There ne'er was woman who'd rebuff strong Biff.
                                        [*Exit Biff.*

GEORGE   My boy, as though I were a wise soothsayer,
I can report thy words ere thou dost speak them—
And thou hast truth in each and ev'ry letter.
Afore thou judgest, though, I bid thee listen;   80
Without reflecting, do not be rejecting.
'Tis very true—Biff is my supervisor,
And while I can compose reports most ably,
I am less skill'd at confrontations, Marty.

MARTY   The car, the car! O Father, he's a knave—   85
He wreck'd the car, destroy'd it utterly.
Great need had I tomorrow of the car.
Didst thou have any notion how important
The night would be to me? Hast e'en a clue?

GEORGE   I did and do and had and have, mine offspring.   90
What may I say to thee but I am sorry?
No other words have I to fix the matter.

Enter LORRAINE, DAVE, *and* LINDA McFLY.
They turn on the television.

MARTY	There is still more: my band shall not perform
	At our school dance, which daily doth approach.
GEORGE	Believe me when I say thou shalt be happy 95
	That thou escap'd the painful aggravation,
	The headaches that, for surety, would follow
	This public exhibition of thy talent—
	It shall but be a torment to your body.
	The dance is but a passing obligation 100
	Thou shalt, in time, be happy to stay clear of.
	Take thou some peanut brittle, ease thy spirit.
MARTY	Not I.
DAVE	—Our father hast it right: the last
	Thing thou dost need is aching of thy head.
GEORGE	Observe the television, which exhibits 105
	Such situations humorous and comic.
	Ha, ha! I chortle ev'ry time I see it.
LORRAINE	This cake I have prepar'd most lovingly,
	Yet we must take its eating on ourselves.
	'Twas fashion'd for thine uncle Joey, who 110
	Did fail again to meet parole conditions
	And shall be gaol'd for another season.
	The bird, alas, shall not take flight today.
	'Twould be most kind if thou wouldst write to him
	Or call to wish him well.
DAVE	—He is thy brother. 115
	Would not the message better come from thee?
LINDA	My brother hath it right while thine is wrong—
	It is a grave embarrassment for us
	To have an uncle who in prison rots
	For all the wrongs that he did perpetrate. 120
LORRAINE	Nay, judge thou not unless thou perfect art—

	All who belong unto the human species	
	Have made mistakes, and lead not blameless lives.
DAVE	O, fie upon it! I am late again.
LORRAINE	Peace, David—hold thy tongue from ev'ry curse,	125
	Lest it may land once more upon thy head.
	Before thou leavest, let me kiss thee once—
	I would bestow protection on thy cheek.
DAVE	Yet quickly, Mother, or I miss my bus.

[Lorraine kisses Dave quickly.

LORRAINE	Upon thy cheek lay I this zealous kiss,	130
	As seal to this example of my love.
DAVE	Farewell, good Father, till we meet again.

[Dave kisses George on the head.

	What ho! The oil thou puttest on thy pate
	Is past its prime and soon shall need a change!
GEORGE	Ha, ha! Mine eldest hath a matchless humor.	135

[Exit Dave.

LINDA	Young brother Marty, I do not purport
	Nor have desire to schedule all thy trysts
	Or be accomplice to thy rendezvous—
	And yet, by kindness of a sister's heart
	I give thee this intelligence: whilst thou	140
	Wert outside pouting o'er our broken car,
	Twice wert thou callèd by thy Jennifer.
LORRAINE	She is no friend of mine, nay, verily,
	A lass who calls a lad doth ask for trouble.
	Belike she would tempt angels unto sin.	145
LINDA	Thine antiquated views, sweet Mother, keep
	Not time with how the modern age doth dance:
	There is no harm to call upon a lad.
LORRAINE	These views, though they be antiquated, shall

Be mine whate'er the music doth require: 150
I ne'er shall move in time with fornication,
Nor dance unto the beat of primal lust.
'Tis terrible, a lass to call a lad,
A girl to chase a boy with siren song.
When I was young, I never chas'd a boy,   155
Ne'er call'd a boy upon the telephone,
Ne'er sat, whilst parking, with a naughty boy,
Engag'd in some impure activity.

LINDA   How shall I, then, meet somebody to love,
               To share the length and wonder of my days?   160

LORRAINE   Kind Fate shall thread the matter carefully.
               It shall be unto thee as 'twas for me,
               When I thy father met so long ago.

LINDA   Nay, 'twas not Fate—it was Grandfather's car
               Which hit my father with a dreadful force.   165

LORRAINE   Nay, for Fate moves in a mysterious way,
               Its wonders to perform. 'Twas meant to be.
               If thy grandfather had not struck him, then
               I'll warrant none of ye had e'er been born.

LINDA   One aspect of the tale, though, doth confuse: 170
               What trade did Father ply that brought him to
               The middle of the street that fateful day?

LORRAINE   What was it, George? Remind me, if thou wilt—
               Wert thou outside to watch a fledgling bird,
               With feathers soft and body round and supple?   175

GEORGE   What sayest thou, Lorraine? Yea, what impliest?

LORRAINE   Whate'er it was, Grandfather hit him then—
               The car did nearly make him carrion—
               And brought the boy inside the house apace.
               Thy father, who was then no father but   180

A helpless boy, and innocent of heart,
Did seem more like a puppy than a man.
My spirit nearly burst to see him ill,
And thus did hurt begin to turn my heart.

LINDA   Thou hast this story told a thousand times,   185
That we, thy children, may recite it, too:
Thou did feel sorry for the bruis'd boy George,
So didst thou go with him unto the dance,
The Happy Fish that Swam Beneath the Sea.

LORRAINE   Thy memory is far more fallible   190
Than thou dost think, dear, for the dance was call'd
Enchantment 'Neath the Sea. Our fond first date,
First evening of romance and courtship sweet,
First memories together, side by side,
First moments of a long life full of love.   195
There was a horrid thunderstorm that night—
Dost thou remember, George? [Aside:] He listens not,
Though somewhere deep within I know he hears.
[To Linda:] 'Twas there, upon the dance floor, that
                                                        same night,
Thy father kiss'd me with a passion strong.   200
Then was it I did know, within my soul,
I would most gladly spend my life with him,
Live by him, day by day, to face the world,
We two a pair of lovers for the ages.
          [George, not listening, laughs at the television.

GEORGE   Ha! Television, what a fine invention,   205
Invention of ingenious, witty people,
Companion true unto my weary moments!
                              [Exeunt all but Lorraine.

LORRAINE   My life hath not unfolded, since that night,

As I had once expected it would go.
Were I an author, writing out a life,   210
I might have put more passion in the tale,
More sweet sensation in the lovers' scenes,
More pure emotion from the gentleman.
My life was writ with far too few surprises,
Too little of the shot of Cupid's bow,   215
Too limited a taste of love's great feast.
Had I the chance to script a page of life,
I would have more of kisses, more of touch,
More of the glances shar'd betwixt a pair
Of lovers who do know each other well.   220
Give me the pen, and I shall write a book
To put the famous tales of love to shame:
Eurydice and Orpheus? No match.
Kind Guinevere and Lancelot? A jest.
Isolde and Tristan? Feeble were their hearts.   225
Proud Paris and his Helen, she of Troy?
My story would outshine those lovers all.
Alas, I am no poet of love lines,
Nor are my days more than quotidian.
Lorraine doth live, not write, a human life,   230
In which she is not lover, nay, but wife.

                                               [*Exit.*

SCENE 4

Twin Pines Mall.

Enter MARTY MCFLY, *sleeping.*
Enter DOCTOR EMMETT BROWN *above,*
on balcony, on the phone.

DOC   Up, Marty, from thy rest, and come apace—
     I hope thou art not sleeping whilst I wait?
        [Marty wakes suddenly and answers the phone.
MARTY   Nay, Doc, not sleep, but something very like.
     I would not leave thee all alone tonight.
DOC   Pray, hear me, Marty: I have quite forgot   5
     The instrument wherewith I may record
     Our goings-on tonight: my camera,
     With video to capture our brave deeds.
     Wilt thou unto my residence anon,

| | Delivering the camera thence to me? | 10 |
MARTY   At once. I'll fail thee not, and see thee soon.

[Exit Doc. Marty rushes to Doc's residence.
The selfsame camera he doth desire
Is here, and I shall bring it unto him,
Upon my trusted skateboard, through the town,
Now unto Twin Pines Mall to hear Doc's plan,   15
With which he hath been recently obsess'd.
What it may prove to be I have no clue,
With Doc, though, ever is it interesting.

Enter EINSTEIN *next to a cargo truck.*

To Twin Pines Mall I come, and one fifteen
Is shown upon the clock that standeth here.   20
There is Doc's truck, and there his loyal dog—
E'en Einstein, smartest canine I do know.
But where of Doc? O Einstein, dost thou know?
Where is thy master, hast thou seen him?
EINSTEIN   —Woof![1]

The back door of the truck opens.
Enter DOCTOR EMMETT BROWN *in a DeLorean car.*

MARTY   What wonder's this? What advent glorious?   25
Unless mine eyes deceive, before me is
The most distinctive silver frame of the

[1] *Editor's translation*: Though I am doglike in mine appetite,
I have no taste, a secret to preempt.
Thus wait, I bid thee, Marty. Soon enow
Thou shalt perceive Doc's brilliance for thyself!

DeLorean—a car most nonpareil.
The future we do glimpse through these machines
Of which I've heard, but I have never seen.   30
E'en so, 'tis clear to me the car is chang'd,
With alterations built for certain tasks.
The plate upon its rear reads "OUTATIME,"
A message of some urgency, perchance,
Or with a deeper meaning yet to grasp?   35
All shall I soon discover, by my troth—
The doors of this, the stunning, four-wheel'd marvel,
Ope upward, like the wings of Pegasus.
Now, flank'd on ev'ry side by smoke and steam,
The figure of Doc Brown comes into view.   40

DOC   My friend, good Marty! Thou art hither come!
MARTY   Nor would I miss this moment, I do swear.
DOC   Thou welcome art to mine experiment—
        The biggest venture I did e'er attempt,
        The one for which I've waited all my life.   45
MARTY   Thou hast, I see, a sleek DeLorean . . .
DOC   Be patient and thy questions shall find answer.
        Begin to make a record of the night,
        And I'll unfurl a story to delight.
MARTY   What dost thou wear? Is it a Devo suit?   50
DOC   Nay, mind thou not—for if a problem comes
        Along, be sure that I shall whip it, Marty.
MARTY   Indeed. Proceed then, I beseech thee, Doc,
        I stand prepar'd, thy genius to record.
        [Marty begins using the video camera to record Doc.
DOC   Friends, makers, countrymen, lend me your ears—   55
        My name ye know: 'tis Doctor Emmett Brown.
        I stand upon the stony parking lot

Of Twin Pines Mall, Hill Valley, California.
It is the early morn of Saturday,
October 26—Saint Crispin's Day   60
Just past—of nineteen hundred eighty-five.
The time upon the clock is one eighteen,
Ante meridiem, to be precise.
Here ye shall witness history, my friends.
Observe my temporal experiment,   65
Which shall be number'd one—the very first.
Come, Einstein, climb inside the shiny car,
Which glows with silver sheen of mercury.

                        [Einstein jumps into the
                             DeLorean's driver's seat.

In now, and sit thee down upon the seat.
Place now, as I assist, the safety belt   70
'Round thy belovèd, shaggy canine hide.
Behold ye, through the lens that doth not lie,
The clocks that Einstein and myself do wear:
Please note that Einstein's clock is synchroniz'd
With this, mine own control watch, twin of his. 75
Canst see it, Marty, through the camera?

MARTY   Forsooth! I see it clearly through the sight.
           Proceed, I pray: thy tale, Doc, would cure deafness.

DOC   Be well, my faithful Einstein. Watch thy head,
           And may thy voyage bear abundant fruit.   80
           [To Marty:] With this remote I'll conquer the remote.

MARTY   I prithee, is't connected to the car?

DOC   Behold, I bid thee, Marty.

MARTY   —As thou wilt.

            [Doc moves the car with the remote control.
           [Aside:] Amazing power, held within his hands!

The potent car doth leap at his command,   85
An 'twere a phantom sat behind the wheel.
By Jove, the thing is fast—across the lot
It spins, with speed like chariot of old
That plung'd from high above when Icarus
Provok'd the gods and tried to touch the sun.   90
Doc, say: what is this power?

DOC   —Film not me,
But keep the focus always on the car!

MARTY   [aside:] The car doth face us, now, across the lot,
And though wise Doc hath park'd it far away,
'Tis ominous—its lights aim'd straight at us   95
As if it had its mind on some revenge
And we two were the target of its ire.
(How its bleak stare reminds me of a tale
About a rank enchantress nam'd Christine.)

DOC   If ev'ry calculation is correct,   100
When this—my baby, source of all my hopes—
Doth hit upon the speed of eighty-eight,
In miles per hour, then Marty, verily,
Thine eyes shalt witness shit most serious.

MARTY   [aside:] The car accelerates yet doth not move, 105
But spins its tires far faster than a cyclone.
It burneth rubber like a mighty pyre
And rocketh back and forth with energy,
Each centimeter itching for release.
The meter Doc doth hold goes up and up   110
And shows the speed potential rising higher—
Ten, twenty, thirty, forty, more than sixty,
E'en fleeter than a cheetah at a sprint.
Doc flips a switch, and now the car doth come!

It groweth closer, like a comet that   115
Doth make its way across the starry heav'ns
And passes through the atmosphere of Earth.
This comet, though, seems bound to hit us both!
The car approacheth quickly, like a bolt,
With Einstein smiling happily inside.   120
I am afeard! Hath Doc his senses lost?
Is mine own friend my doom?

DOC   —Fear not. Behold!
The time is near—soon thou shalt wonders see.

MARTY   Past seventy, past eighty! Then, a flash!
White light surrounds us, brighter than the sun.   125

> [The car, approaching them quickly,
> disappears as it travels through time.

What's this? A trick? A jest? The car is gone!
And in its wake, a pair of flaming tracks.

DOC   Ha, ha! What hath I said to thee, my friend?
'Tis eighty-eight in miles per hour, forsooth!
The temporal displacement hath occurr'd   130
Precisely on the clock stroke of one twenty
And zero seconds!

MARTY   —Zounds! The car is gone!
Naught doth remain except the metal plate,
Which burneth me as I do pick it up.
O "OUTATIME," what doth your message mean?   135
This wondrous night entire is out of time,
And out of sense, and out of all belief.
What hast thou fashion'd, Doc? Is Einstein slain,
Disintegrated in a million pieces?

DOC   Naught is disintegrated, Marty, nay!   140
Take heart and be thou calm—I shall explain.

Each molecule and bit of Einstein and
The car itself are utterly intact.

MARTY   Intact, yet disappear'd? Hell's fire, good Doc!
Where are they, if not here before our eyes?   145

DOC   Thy question's not appropriately ask'd:
'Tis not the "where," my friend, it is the "when."
My loyal Einstein hath, e'en here, become
The first time traveler the world hath known.
He hath been sent into the future! See?   150
One minute in the future, by my troth.
When 'tis one twenty-one and zero seconds,

	Our time shall reach where he already is—	
	Where Einstein and the time machine are both.	
MARTY	For my part, I am so attir'd in wonder,	155
	I know not what to say. Yet, prithee, speak:	
	Dost thou tell me thou built a time machine	
	Inside the frame of a DeLorean?	
	Was ever science in this humor plied?	
	Was ever science in this humor won?	160
DOC	As I perceive the matter, if one shall	
	Create a time machine out of a car,	
	Then wherefore not fulfill the task with style?	
	Some matters practical give reason, too—	
	The stainless-steel construction of the car	165
	Doth make the flux dispersal—[*his watch beeps*] O,	
	take heed!	

[*Doc pushes Marty aside as the car
reappears, skidding to a halt.*

MARTY	[*aside:*] Ah, me, that I were still at home abed.	
DOC	The car doth rock and creak and blow forth smoke,	
	As if it had experienc'd a storm	
	And was the worse for wear. I'll ope the door.	170
	Alack! A foul idea.	
MARTY	—Why? Is it hot?	
	For as it steameth so, methinks must be.	
DOC	Nay, nay, 'tis cold, like Satan's heart itself.	
	My boot I shall employ to do the deed.	

[*Doc opens the door with his foot.*

EINSTEIN   Woof, woof![2]
DOC   —O, Einstein, wondrous animal!   175
             Behold his clock and mine, the twain are split—
             His runs behind, one minute after mine.
             Yet both still tick, maintaining movements true.
MARTY   The dog, it seems, hath liv'd.
DOC   —The dog is well!
             Completely unaware of what hath been—   180
             In his experience, the trip was smooth,
             A journey instantaneous, indeed.
             Thus is his clock one minute after mine:
             He hath that minute skipp'd, and instantly
             Arriv'd upon this bank and shoal of time.   185
             Come hither, and I'll show thee how it works.
MARTY   I shall, for more of this I'd gladly know.
                              [Doc and Marty approach the car.
DOC   First, one must activate the time circuits.
             Three screens display the when that thou shalt go:

---

[2]   *Editor's translation*: The warp and woof of time I have travers'd
      And come out on the other side intact.
      The car convey'd me quickly through the lot—
      I plummeted toward both Doc and Marty,
      Afraid I, peradventure, would come crashing
      Into these gentlemen whom I adore,
      And in so doing break my canine heart.
      Instead, it seem'd a lightning bolt did strike,
      As though 'twere thrown by some Olympian god.
      A sudden, deep sensation fill'd my bones,
      Like tingling—from my pate unto my tail,
      My paws unto the middle of my back—
      The flash subsided, and the men had mov'd,
      Away from danger, as though by some magic.
      Did e'er a dog enjoy so strange a life?
      Was e'er a master as astute as mine?

The first one tells thee whither thou art bound, 190
The second telleth thee whence thou art come,
The third doth tell the where and when thou wert.
Thou must upon this simple keypad put
The time of thine intended destination.
Wouldst thou bear witness to the signing of 195
The Declaration of an Independence?
'Twould be July the fourth, of seventeen
And sev'nty-six. Mayhap thou wouldst prefer
To be a magus at the birth of Christ?
Thou shouldst put in December twenty-fifth 200
When anno Domini itself began!
What of this date, red-letter, I recall,
Within the very history of science?
November fifth, of nineteen fifty-five?
E'en as I type the code, the memories 205
Rush turbulently to my brain and do
Fill up my mind, like water in a tub.
November fifth, of nineteen fifty-five!
The verse itself doth spring into my mind:
[*Reciting:*] Remember, remember, 210
The fifth of November,
      'Twas my flux capacitor thought—
There's no reason or rhyme
Why the travel through time
      Should ever be forgot. 215

MARTY   What is it, Doc? For I do know it not.
DOC   'Twas then I first time travel did conceive.
        How vividly the mem'ry of that day
        Comes swooping, birdlike, to my agèd mind.
        I stood, far too unsteady and unsure, 220

Upon the precipice of my commode.
'Twas my intent to fix a timepiece there,
High on the wall above my humble throne.
The porcelain was wet, as was its wont,
Which caus'd my feet to slip and me to fall.   225
My head did meet the sink with knock immense,
And there I lay, unconscious on the floor.
Yet whether fall or fate, thou canst decide:
For, as I woke, a vision came to me—
Sent by, no doubt, some saint of blessèd science   230
While flights of angels sang me to my best.
The vision was a revelation pure,
Wherein I saw the future—and the past!—
Available e'en to a human grasp.
I saw a picture blazon'd on my mind: 235
A picture I would earnestly pursue,
A picture I would chase for thirty years,
A picture that was worth a thousand words,
A picture that gave unto me my aim,
My lifelong work: the flux capacitor.   240

MARTY   What is this wondrous flux capacitor?
DOC   Near thirty years and all my fam'ly's fortune
        I've spent to see the vision of that day.
        O heavens, hath so long a time elaps'd?
        They do speak true who utter "tempus fugit,"   245
        And "carpe diem" also, by my troth.
        Within those years, there's much hath chang'd nearby—
        How I remember when this all was farmland,
        Far as the eye could see or voice could shout.
        'Twas old man Peabody who own'd this plot.   250
        A character most strange: he ever wish'd

	To breed varieties of pine trees here.	
MARTY	O heavy times, begetting such events!	
	This is fantastical to the extreme.	
	The car—say more of it, Doc—doth it run	255
	On regular unleaded gasoline?	
DOC	Unfortunately, nay. It doth require	
	A substance with a stronger kick, indeed—	
	Plutonium, though rare and dangerous,	
	Doth power this miraculous machine.	260
MARTY	Beg pardon? For I heard "plutonium,"	
	Which must not be the word that thou hast us'd.	
	Is't possible mine ears have heard aright?	
	Dost thou report this craft is nuclear?	
DOC	Film further, for mine answer is important.	265
	Nay, nay, the splendid craft's electrical—	
	Yet it requires a nuclear reaction	
	To generate the mighty current of	
	The one point twenty-one in gigawatts	
	Of pow'r electrical that I do need.	270
MARTY	Yet Doc, unless mine information's poor,	
	One may not purchase at a local market	
	A vial of plutonium to use;	
	Th'unstable element is far too scarce.	
	Pray, tell me true: hast thou the substance filch'd?	275
DOC	Forsooth! I stole it from a rotten group	
	Of nationalists, they of Libya.	
	They did pursue my special services	
	And bid me make a rank, destroying bomb,	
	With which who knows what villainy they'd ply?	280
	I took their treasure—their plutonium—	
	And did present them with a bomb most false,	

Mere casing with a pinball's parts inside.
Was not this clever? Quickly, find a suit
That shall protect thee from the radiation.   285
The car we shall reload, and travel more.

MARTY   [aside:] Doc stole plutonium? All is not well.
I doubt some foul play. Would the night were o'er!
Till then sit still, my soul. Foul deeds will rise,
Though all the Earth o'erwhelm them, to our eyes.   290

                    [Marty dons a radiation suit
                    while Doc picks up the plutonium.

DOC   Most carefully this matter must I handle,
Else shall the matter end most grievously.
Within the waiting tube cylindrical
I shall deposit this plutonium.
A twist most gentle and at once it flies—   295

            [The plutonium is sucked into the DeLorean.

With hearty appetite the car hath ta'en it.
Now all is safe—the chamber's lin'd with lead.
The tapes thou hast recorded on this night
I bid thee guard them carefully, my friend.
We shall need record of this fateful night.   300
I am prepar'd to travel once again,
To venture 'cross the passageways of time,
If I, despite my scatter'd, anxious thoughts
My luggage can remember ere I go.
'Twould be most humorous if I appear'd   305
Sans undergarments in a future time.
Who knoweth if the future still doth use
The cotton underwear of which I'm fond?
I shall progress, not be undress'd or stress'd.
Then shall my allergy unto synthetics   310

	Not be a hindrance to my synthesis	
	Of time and space, of present, past, and future.	
MARTY	The future? Is it then that thou art bound?	
DOC	Yea, Marty, verily. 'Tis mine intent	
	Anon to travel twenty-five years hence.	315
	Long have I dream'd of witnessing the future,	
	Of seeing moments far beyond my years.	
	I long to see the path of humankind,	
	And what advances our shrewd race hath made.	
MARTY	And wherefore not? Thou hast the means to do it.	320
DOC	So many small discoveries I'll make—	
	Not just the serious developments,	
	But also those quotidian delights	
	That make a human life enjoyable.	
	For instance, I shall learn which baseball teams	325
	Become World Series champs through twenty-ten.	
	[Aside:] At least, methinks, by then the Cubs must win.	
MARTY	If I a small request might make, my friend,	
	Wouldst thou look in on me when thou arriv'st?	
DOC	I shall, and would not miss thee for the world.	330
	I prithee, roll once more the video.	

                           [Marty resumes recording.
                    Doc opens the door of the DeLorean.

	I, Doctor Emmett Brown, shall soon embark	
	Upon a journey of historic scope.	
	A-ha! What folly! I had near forgot	
	To bring an excess of plutonium	335
	With which I shall come safely home again.	
	How should I make return without its strength?	
	One pellet for one trip! I am most mad.	

EINSTEIN	Woof![3]
DOC	—Wherefore art thou barking, Einie?
EINSTEIN	—Woof![4]

DOC   My God. They found me. How, I do not know,   340
        And yet 'tis clear they found me nonetheless.
        An 'twere I were a needle in a haystack
        Which they had found, and soon would thread the eye.
        Nay, nay, it cannot be. Run, Marty, Run!

MARTY   Who is it who hath found thee? Tell me, Doc!   345

DOC   Whom dost thou think? The frightful Libyans!

Enter two LIBYANS *in a van.*

LIBYAN 1   [*aside:*] When ye behold me, see no enemy.
           And neither let thy bias typecast me,
           And call me monster, villainous and crude.
           My homeland, which I love, is quite a marvel,   350
           A culture beautiful and flourishing.
           Our Tuareg music sends our feet to dance—
           Our pipes resound in stirring melodies,
           With drums that mark the beating of our hearts.
           How I love feasts of shorba and bazeen,   355
           Prepar'd the way my family did eat them,
           Made from tomatoes red as summer sun.
           Our country is a home to the Sahara,
           The desert of a thousand tales and songs,
           Whose vast, forbidding sandbanks are renown'd.   360
           My country's skies are bluer than the ocean,

---

[3] *Editor's translation*: Behold, my master, someone doth approach.
[4] *Editor's translation*: Look there, toward the entrance of the lot!

And sunlight beameth on Aleppo pine.
But other lands have sunlight, too. Moreover,
The skies are everywhere as blue as mine.
O hear my song, thou God of all the nations,   365
A song of peace for their land and for mine.
Nay, call me not an enemy, my friend,
For I am one who'd gladly welcome peace.
Yet when the time for peace hath fled and gone,
When others do betray us wrongfully,   370
Shall we not act? Hath not a Libyan eyes?
Hath not a Libyan his hands and organs,
Dimensions, senses, passions, and affections?
Fed with the same food, hurt with the same weapons,
And subject to the same diseases, heal'd   375
By the same means, both warm'd and coolèd, too,
By the same winter and same summer as
Yourselves? If you prick us, do we not bleed?
Or if you tickle us, do we not laugh?
Yea, if you poison us, do we not die?   380
And if you wrong us, shall we not revenge?
                    [*The Libyans begin shooting at Doc and Marty.*

MARTY   Alas! We two are in a quagmire now.
                    They strike at us with murderous intent.
DOC   I'll lead them hence and draw their fire away!
MARTY   Nay, Doc, attempt thou no heroic deeds.   385
                                    [*The Libyans corner Doc.*
DOC   The gun I hold within my trembling hand
                    I throw aside. (For lo, it worketh not.)
                                    [*Doc tosses his gun.*
                    If ye have hearts, I plead—I beg—for mercy.
                    The quality of mercy is not strain'd,

It droppeth as the gentle rain from heaven   390
Upon the place beneath. Its pow'r is greatest
When mercy seasons justice.

LIBYAN 1   —Justice 'tis.
                    [Libyan 1 shoots Doc, who dies.

MARTY   Nay! Bastard base!

LIBYAN 1   —Why bastard? Wherefore base?

MARTY   Although my works bespeak my bravery,
             I must turn tail and flee, or end like Doc.   395
                    [Marty is cornered by the Libyans.
             Mine end is near. Farewell, cruel life, and short!
                    *[Libyan 1's gun jams. Libyan 2 fails to start
                                             their van.*
             Spar'd for another moment, yet to live.
             Unto the car I'll fly, which shall convey
             Me faster than my feet could ever flee.

LIBYAN 1   This Russian gun, fie!

LIBYAN 2   —Foh, this German van!   400

LIBYAN 1   Get hence, that we may kill the young one, too.
                         [The van drives once more.
                   Marty climbs in the DeLorean to drive away,
                         and the Libyans begin chasing Marty.
MARTY   Shut thou the door, and swiftly, Marty, too,
              Or else these moments few may be thy last.
              My friend, my Doc, is murder'd 'fore mine eyes,
              And I shall join him if I do not flee.   405
              He was a kind man, generous of heart,
              Who had a mind inventive and astute—
              A bit outrageous, yea, but such are they
              Who would create a future none can see.
              Not since the war wherein brave Hector fell,   410
              Pursu'd by harsh Achilles to the death,
              Did such a foe chase down a hero good.
              I shall not let them beat me, too, herein,
              That they may desecrate my body as
              The mean Achaeans did to Hector's corpse.   415
              Drive now, DeLorean, and keep me safe,
              Bear me away from these bleak men apace.
              They shoot at me, yet—happ'ly—miss the mark.
              These gears of this machine I quickly shift,
              And as I do the screens and instruments   420
              Light up, though I've no time to read their meaning.
              Still—in the rearview mirror—I can see
              Them fiddling with their guns to end my life.
              I parry, dodge, and drive e'en faster yet,
              To keep their bullets from their target—me!   425
              Yet faster, car, drive on, be fleet of wheel,
              Like chariots of fire leave all behind
              And in a blaze of glory help me 'scape.

The speed ascendeth—sixty, seventy,
Ne'er have I, on our highways, driven thus.   430
In tales of derring-do and pure adventure
A thrilling chase is oft the centerpiece.
As I have watch'd these stories, they excite,
Yet in the living it is far more fright'ning
To be the hunted in a scene of fear.   435
Now, looking back once more do I espy
A mighty cannon, which they have prepar'd
To work me woe, destroy me utterly.
I name it, simply, horrifying death,
The reaper that hath come for young McFly.   440
By all that's holy, I am sore afeard,
Yet courage does not mean one's not afraid,
But standeth strong against the fear, forsooth.
E'en thus I stand, and ready for this fight:
Control shall shift, and I shall here prevail.   445
I challenge ye, you wretched, filthy foes,
Unto a race—the wager, mine own life.
Not since the tortoise and the wayward hare
Will such a race earn such a lasting fame.
Let's see if your weak van may yet attain   450
The lightning speed of ninety miles per hour!
Pray hear the motto of mine ancestors:
"*Nolite te bastardes carborund'rum*!"
Yet even as I do accelerate
Those words of Doc most clearly I recall: 455
At eighty-eight in miles per hour measur'd,
A wondrous thing shall happen, shall it not?
The thought doth come but hazily to mind,
For thoughts of mere survival fill my head.

Yet what is this—a sudden flash, a light,   460
An 'twere a million stars did shine at once
And I were in the center of their pull.
'Tis time! The time hath come, the time hath gone!
Surrender, Marty, to this blazing light,
That thou mayst live again another night!   465

                                        [Exeunt.

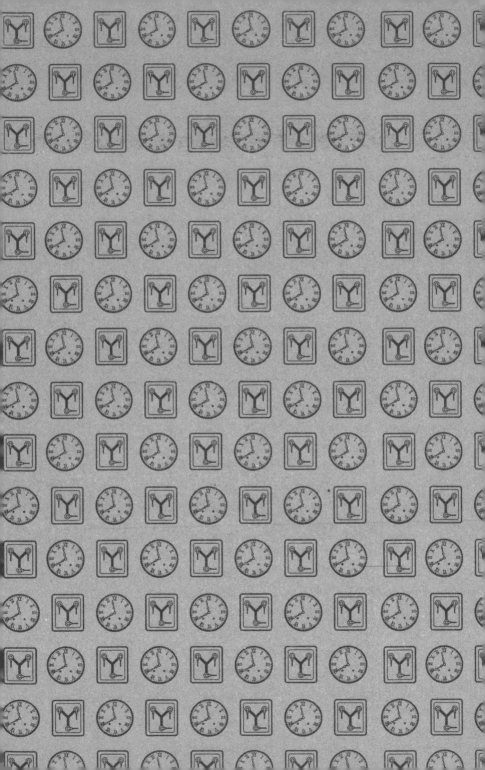

ACT II

SCENE 1

The year 1955. At the Peabody farm.

Enter PA PEABODY. *Enter* MA, SHERMAN,
and SIS PEABODY, *aside.*

PA   There ne'er was person steady as a tree—
No man so rooted to the stable ground,
No woman with a stump so strong and stout,
No people with their branches lifted up
Whilst, sensibly, their trunk was planted fast.   5
All trees are noble, wise, and solid, too,
Be they deciduous or evergreen.
And while I am a friend to ev'ry tree,
A pine tree is a human's truest friend.
The pine tree is a paragon of virtue,   10
Example true of miracles divine.
Each branch stands for a possibility,
Each needle a perfection rob'd in green.
A pine shall never fail you or betray,
Shall never gossip or put forth a lie,   15
Or give you reason e'er to doubt its heart.
A pine tree doth give answer to your work—
The tender maintenance you give to it—
With growth each year: astounding, beautiful.
Give me a pine to tend, with bark and sap,   20
With all the precious glory of its kind,
And you shall find a happy Peabody.

Enter MARTY MCFLY, *appearing in the DeLorean.*

MARTY	Where am I now? This field, this scarecrow, too,
	Where is the parking lot where I was driving?
	What is this barn? I plunge, I crash, alack! 25
	[The DeLorean crashes into
	Pa Peabody's barn. The Peabodys
	rush to the barn to look at the car.
MA	What is this eerie apparition, Pa?
	Methinks its lights do glow like hell's own fire.
PA	It hath th'appearance of an airplane, dear,
	Yet hath no wing parts wherewith it may fly.
SHERMAN	Nay, 'tis no airplane. Look! Behold this book. 30
	Hath not this gadget the appearance of
	A flying object, unidentified,
	Wherein a spaceman comes to sack the Earth?
	Space zombies come from Pluto in't, belike.
	[The door of the DeLorean opens, revealing
	Marty in his radiation suit and helmet.
MA	Alas!
PA	—Run quickly, Ma, and fetch my musket! 35
	[The Peabodys run from the barn,
	and Pa grabs his gun.
MARTY	I am mistaken. Pray, scream not at me!
	A lonesome traveler and much perplex'd
	I am, but wish no harm to come to ye!
	[Aside:] They all have fled, and I am left alone
	With these few cows who call the barn their home. 40
	I must attempt to make some sense of this.
	[Calling out:] What ho, good citizens! I mean no harm,
	And sorry am I for thy lovely barn

That lately I have wreck'd with this, my car.
              [Marty emerges from the
              barn and Pa shoots at him.

SHERMAN Already doth the wicked beast mutate,   45
         Into a human form. O Father, shoot!
              [Marty retreats into the barn.

PA   Die, alien—our planet is not thine,
         Thou mutant son of wenches most impure!
              [Marty bursts from the
              barn driving the DeLorean.

SHERMAN It flees within its spaceship, like a fiend!
PA   Hold, monster, thou shalt not defile my land.   50
MARTY   *[aside:]* Enow of shooting and of threats have I,
         And would not face another e'er again.
         Where is the peaceful life, which once I led?
         Now all is bullets and horrific strife.
              [The DeLorean smashes a pine tree
              as it drives away from the farm.

PA   Nay, not my precious pine! O, naughty knave—   55
         Space bastard hideous, thou kill'dst my pine!
              [Exeunt Peabodys.

MARTY   Take simple breaths, McFly, all is not lost.
         This must be but a dream, and nothing more—
         A most intense and strange and awful dream.
         Alas! What is this sign before mine eyes?   60
         Stop, car! I must outside to see it clearly.
              [Marty steps out of the car.
         These pillars I have seen a thousand times
         As I unto my neighborhood arriv'd.
         My parents' home in this development
         Doth stand and always hath—Estates of Lyon.   65

Two matching lions lie upon the blocks,
Like monarchs of the forest keeping watch.
Yet now, beyond those pillars, nothing is—
No streets, no homes, no neighborhood of mine.
Is this some trick, some odd hallucination?   70
Bulldozers only, and a road of dirt,
Are all that do remain of mine own home.
Aside I see another sign, which may
Provide some context to mine aching mind.
"Live in tomorrow's home today," it sayeth.   75

                    Enter two SENIOR CITIZENS *in a car.*

          Good gentles, can you help me? Please, I beg.
OLD LADY Nay, do not stop, sweet Wilbur, drive thou on—
          This stranger, strangely clad, shall be our end!
                              [Exeunt senior citizens.
MARTY   That car was classic, from another time.
          Not from my era, nay, but older far   80
          This cannot be, 'tis madness, pure and simple.
                              [Marty tries to start
                              the DeLorean, and it stalls.
          Now doth the car e'en fail me—O, perfection:
          A perfect muddle into which I've fallen.
          What beeping's here? A sensor doth report
          The car is missing its plutonium.   85
          Of course, for if 'tis all as I suspect,
          The rare plutonium hath been us'd up
          As I did make a backward jump in time.
          Then I must be in nineteen fifty-five,
          However doubtful such a truth may be.   90

I'll push the car behind this billboard large,
That none may find the thing and pilfer it.
This sign upon the road doth say Hill Valley
Is but a two-mile walk away from here.
Howe'er unlikely this scenario,   95
Though time would trap me, I'll not have it so.

                                               [Exit.

SCENE 2

In the town of Hill Valley.

Enter various RESIDENTS OF HILL VALLEY.
A car passes by with RED THOMAS'*s image upon it.*
An announcer on the RADIO *can be heard from within the car.*

RADIO   [*in car:*] Elect again our baron, good Red Thomas,
              For truly, progress is his middle name.
              His progress platform meaneth more employment,
              Improvèd education for the young,
              Improvements civic, and reduc'd taxation.   5
              I bid thee, when election day doth come,
              Cast your votes for a trusted, proven leader!

The car leaves. Enter MARTY MCFLY *from the same direction.*

MARTY   [*aside:*] What sights I've seen since I did here arrive—
              This is Hill Valley, town where I reside,

And yet undoubtedly 'tis chang'd as well.   10
The music I hear playing is no song
Of modern times, but something from the past.
The tale of Mister Sandman and how he
Assisteth in the work of bringing dreams:
This drowsy Cupid—Eros, by the Greeks—   15
Doth use no arrows but a sleeping draught
To lull a paramour to loving sleep.
The song enchanted thirty years ago,
Yet now it soundeth old to youthful ears.
The films our nearby theater doth screen   20
Are also from the bygone days of yore—
The Stanwyck/Reagan western that it shows
Doth sound to me more like a voting platform;
The Reagan that I know doth lead our nation.
The cars are classic, from another time,   25
The people, too, array'd as once they were
In photos of a history now past.
The service station seemeth heaven sent—
A bell dings playfully as cars approach
And men—like bees upon a fragrant flower—   30
Do swarm to help the customer at once.
'Tis all familiar, yea, yet unfamiliar.
A car did pass with message to convey:
To reelect the baron—one Red Thomas—
Whom I know not, of whom I've never heard.   35
Moreover, whilst I stood dumbstruck and gap'd,
The clock—the very clock which should be broken—
Began to chime as it has never done,
Not in my lifetime, nay. Its mournful tone,
Westminster, is a deep and soulful knell   40

That shakes me to my core. Last scene of all,
That ends this strange eventful history,
Was one newspaper someone did discard,
Which had the current date upon its masthead:
November fifth of nineteen fifty-five.   45
My previous opinion I repeat:
This must be some strange dream, and nothing more.
O'er yonder is, perhaps, mine only hope:
A public telephone in a café,
Wherewith I may find Doc, who should be here,   50
Wherever—or whenever—I may be.

> *[Marty enters the café.*

Enter LOU CARUTHERS *and* CUSTOMERS
of Lou's Café, including young GEORGE MCFLY.
Enter GOLDIE WILSON *aside, working.*

LOU   What is thy story, junior? What hast done—
             Hast thou jump'd from a ship and wander'd here?
MARTY   What, sir?
LOU   —The life preserver thou dost wear
             An 'twere a doublet, yet 'tis surely not,   55
             For never was there doublet so absurd.
MARTY   Forgive me, I would use thy phone. 'Tis all.
LOU   'Tis in the back.
MARTY   —My thanks, kind sir, for this.
                   *[Marty walks to the phone and searches the
                                  phone book for Doc Brown.*
             A phone book, ah! Familiar tome, indeed.
             At least this trusty, critical device   60
             Shall ne'er be out of fashion in the future!

Ah, Brown, so many people have the name—
As if the rainbow had been melted down
And smelted, leaving only that dark hue
To represent the spectrum. Here it is!   65
One Emmett Brown, a scientist, who doth
Reside at sixteen forty Riv'rside Drive.
Hurrah that thou art here and art alive!
I call, but only ringing do I hear,
An endless ringing mocking all my hopes.   70
Alack! I'll take this page with his address,
To find him with my feet, if nothing else.
[*To Lou:*] Know'st thou where sixteen forty Riverside—

LOU Shalt thou some morsel order, wayward lad?

MARTY Indeed. Give me a Tab.

LOU   —A tab thou'lt have   75
Once thou dost place thine order. Know'st thou not
How this doth work in modern times as these?

MARTY A Pepsi Free, then, prithee, shall be mine.

LOU No Pepsi free! Thou must pay for thy drink.

MARTY [*aside:*] The man doth turn my words in baffling

                                                circles 80
As if they were a top and he the spinner.
[*To Lou:*] Give me some drink that hath no sugar, yea?
'Tis all I ask of thee.

                         [*Marty sits next to George*
                           but does not notice him.

LOU   —Aught lacking sugar.
Thou art a puzzling and a naughty lad.
I'll give thee coffee black, with sugar none.   85

Enter young BIFF TANNEN *with* SKINHEAD, 3-D, *and* MATCH.

BIFF   Thou imp, McFly! What art thou at herein?
                        [Both Marty and George
                        turn their heads toward Biff.

MARTY   *[quietly:]* Biff Tannen, by my troth, yet young and
                                                strong.

BIFF   *[to George:]* I speak to thee, McFly, thou Irish pest.

GEORGE   Holla there, Biff, and sirrahs all, hello!
                        [Marty gawks at George.

BIFF   Hast thou my homework finish'd yet, McFly?   90

GEORGE   In truth, it is not yet completed, Biff.
            Because it is not due until far later—
                        [Biff grabs George and
                        begins knocking on his head.

BIFF   I'll bash thee on thy pate, an thou so speakest!
            Are brains herein, that I must knock and see?
            Use thou thy mind and with it think, McFly—   95
            I must have time enow to write the words
            In mine own hand, as if the work were mine.
            Hast thou the consequence consider'd, George,
            Should I submit some homework penn'd by thee,
            Writ in the manner of thy shaky hand?   100
            I would, most quickly, be sent from the school.
            Thou wouldst not want that lot for Biff, wouldst thou?
            Wouldst thou? Speak faster, for thy pause doth vex.

GEORGE   Of course not, Biff, 'twould be a tragedy.
                        [Biff notices Marty staring at George.

BIFF   *[to Marty:]* Upon what lookest thou, thou arse-like
                                                pate? 105

SKINHEAD   Behold his life preserver, Biff—ha, ha!
            This knave, this rogue, this dork thinks he shall drown.

GEORGE   Ha! *[Aside:]* If I laugh, belike they'll let me be.

BIFF	About the homework I require, McFly.
GEORGE	Forsooth, Biff, I shall finish it tonight. 110
	Deliv'ring it to thee upon the morrow.
	Shall this suffice?
BIFF	—It shall, but not too early—
	My wont on Sundays is to slumber late.
	O—look below, McFly, thy shoe's untied.
	[*George looks down and Biff slaps him.*
	Thou art too gullible by thrice, McFly. 115
	Now, as I leave, hear thou these final words:
	I would not see thy face herein again.
GEORGE	Biff, what a wondrous person. Ta, farewell!
	[*Exeunt Biff, Skinhead, 3-D, and Match.*
	George continues eating while Marty stares.
MARTY	[*aside:*] Amazing sight—my father—O, 'tis he!
GEORGE	What is it? For thy stares are like two knives, 120
	Which slice the air and pierce my very visage.
MARTY	By all the heavens—thou art George McFly!
GEORGE	Indeed, yet who art thou that I should care?
GOLDIE	[*approaching:*] Now wherefore shouldst thou let those
	naughty boys
	Push thee around as though thou wert their
	plaything? 125
GEORGE	They bigger are than I, and if thou seest,
	They number four, whilst I am only one.
GOLDIE	Stand tall and proud, my boy, have more respect
	For he whom thou shouldst most respect: thyself.
	Dost thou not know? If, in the present time, 130
	Thou now allowest folk to tread on thee,
	Thy life entire shall folk repeat the walk,
	And thou shalt live thy whole life underfoot.

	Look thou on me—think'st thou that I shall spend
	My days entire within this slop house bleak?	135
LOU	Pray watch thy tongue now, Goldie.
GOLDIE	—Nay, not I!
	I shall make something better of myself.
	My dreams shall take me far—to night school now,
	And in the future I'll somebody be.
MARTY	Indeed! 'Tis right! The man shall baron be!	140
GOLDIE	Yea, I shall—[*aside:*] baron, what a pleasant thought!
	[*To all:*] I shall be baron, ha! So shall it be,
	This strangely cladded soothsayer is right.
	A fine idea, which well doth please my mind.
LOU	A baron with a skin of color, nay—	145
	This is a future I'll not live to see.
GOLDIE	I bid thee, watch me closely, Sir Caruthers—
	I've work'd on jobs with my feet and my hands
	But all my work was for the other man!
	Now I've a chance to do things for myself;	150
	No more I'll beat my head against the wall.
	I shall be baron, the most pow'rful man
	In all Hill Valley. I'll clean up this town!
LOU	'Tis well. Begin by sweeping of the floor.

[Lou hands Goldie a mop. Exit Lou.
Exit George severally.

GOLDIE	It soundeth sweet: thy baron, Goldie Wilson!	155
	Most amply would it suit my fervent goals,
	The worthy heart and soul I do possess,
	With needed progress for Hill Valley, too—
	The town that I do love, which must yet grow.

[Exit Goldie.

| MARTY | Where hast my father—George McFly—escap'd? | 160 |

There, there, outside the window, doth he fly
Atop his bicycle, with chiming bell!
How quickly he eludes discovery,
As if he were engag'd in some foul deed.
I'll follow him, not let him disappear,   165
For gladly would I meet someone I know
In this mysterious, confusing past.
E'en someone awkward and unsure, like Father.
(And, verily, what damage could it do
To make acquaintance with a person whom   170
I shall, hereafter, come to know so well?)
What ho, Dad! George! Thou who dost ride the bike!
I bid thee, stop! Cease all thy pedaling!
Fie, neither ears nor heart do heed my call—
He heareth not, so I must follow on.   175

        [Exit Marty, chasing after George.

Enter GEORGE MCFLY *above, on balcony.*

GEORGE   With these binoculars I shall espy
A woman at her leisure, being dress'd.
Such sight doth stimulate, arouse, excite—
She is the Muse who sparks creative thought,
One of the nine who thus may move men's hearts.   180
The finest of her sisters: skin like silk,
And pink like tulips at the height of spring.
Forfend me, Fate, that she turn not to siren
And dash poor George's life upon the rocks.
I bid ye, gentles, who may see me here,   185
Atop this bough, where I do bow to her—
Who is the paragon of my desire—

Think not that I am proud of what I do.
He who is proud eats up himself: pride is
His glass, his trumpet, his own chronicle.   190
No place hath pride amid necessity,
And this sweet sight, I tell ye verily,
Is more than necessary unto me.

Enter MARTY McFLY.

MARTY   Behold, here is the bike, and there the man!
             Up in a tree and gazing on a house.   195
             The man is nothing but a Peeping Tom,
             Who could not from Godiva draw his eyes.
             Instead, he did behold her nakedness
             As she atop her gallant steed rode on,
             And was, for this offensive act, struck blind.   200
             Nay, George, I bid thee be thou not a Tom—
             Tom George should be another's name, not thine.
             Be careful, sir, lest thou wouldst share his fate
             And find thyself a punish'd, blinded man.
GEORGE   Alack, I slip, I fall!

GEORGE *falls from the balcony.*
Enter SAM BAINES, *driving a car toward him.*

MARTY   —Nay, Father, nay!   205
             Shall my prediction happen in a trice?
             Nay, not while I have life and breath to stop't,
             As sure as I have a thought or a soul.
                    [*Marty pushes George out of the way and is
                              struck by the car. Exit George.*

SAM   Another youth hath jump'd athwart my car!
           What is it with these modern, foolish boys,   210
           E'er seeking for an automotive death?
           'Tis like each doth believe he is James Dean,
           Who was, of late, lost in a tragic crash.
           Would ev'ry young man seek a fate like his,
           That they may die as rebels sans a cause?   215
           [*Calling:*] Pray, Stella, quickly come, wheree'er thou
                                                            art—
           Come hither, we shall take him to the house!
           [*Aside:*] O, for a swifter, more responsive spouse.
                                                    [*Exeunt.*

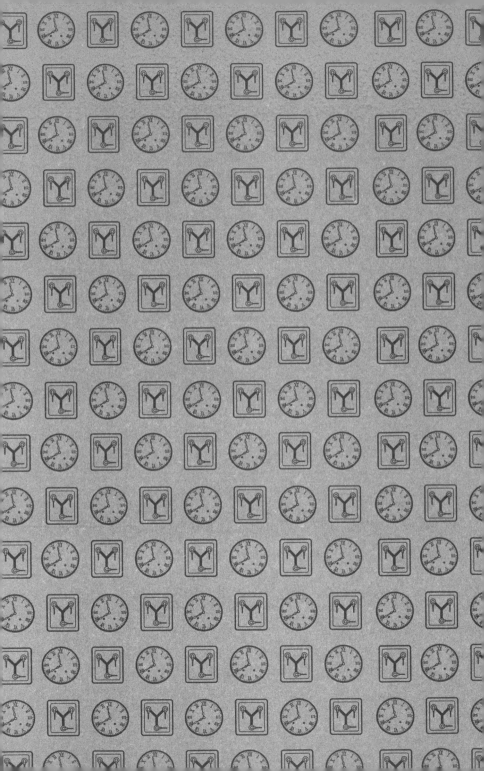

ACT III

SCENE 1

At the Baines house.

Enter young LORRAINE BAINES.
Enter MARTY McFLY *aside, in bed. It is dark.*

LORRAINE	In all my childhood hopes and girlish dreams,
	Ne'er did I think the angels would deliver
	A man unto my house, my room, my bed!
	Such riches almost are too much abundance.
	Yet I shall manage, for this injur'd youth 5
	Is muscular and shapely, like a Greek,
	And I, like Circe, shall give him my welcome.
MARTY	[*waking:*] O Mother, art thou there? I hear thy voice.
LORRAINE	Be still, my dear, relax. Thou hit thy head,
	And hast been sleeping near enow nine hours. 10
MARTY	A nightmare horrible was mine this night,
	Wherein I was a trav'ler, back in time.
	Such hideous things I saw, that with the sight
	I trembling wak'd, and for a season after
	Could not believe but that I was in hell, 15
	Such terrible impression made the dream.
LORRAINE	Thy dream is over; thou art safe and sound
	Back in the year of nineteen fifty-five.
MARTY	What folly speak'st thou? Nineteen fifty-five!

> [*Lorraine turns on a light.*

O eyes, can it be true? Thou art my m— 20
[*Aside:*] Yet how to end this word? Is this my mother?
Belike misapprehension or mirage?

	My mirror, my misunderstanding? Fie!
LORRAINE	My name is call'd Lorraine. Lorraine Baines, I.
MARTY	Ma'am, so thou art, I see. Yet can it be?

25

Forsooth, this must be some peculiar dream.
Lorraine, 'tis thee, and yet it is not thee,
Ne'er have I seen thee passing . . . thin . . . as this.

LORRAINE	Be calm, I bid thee, Calvin. Thou hast earn'd

A bruise upon thy pate for thy brave deeds.

30

| MARTY | I would be gone, but whither flew my pants? |
| LORRAINE | Just there, atop my hope chest, yea, wherein |

I place the articles of my desire.
Thou teachest me new things, good Calvin, for
I never have seen purple underwear.

35

| MARTY | Say, wherefore hast thou call'd me Calvin twice? |
| LORRAINE | Is't not thy name? Art thou call'd Calvin Klein? |

For on thine underwear it is display'd.

[She reaches for the blanket as if to reveal
Marty's underwear.

MARTY   [*aside:*] My codpiece is not thine for viewing, lass.
LORRAINE   Belike thou art call'd Cal. Is this the case?   40
MARTY   Nay, people call me Marty. 'Tis my name.
LORRAINE   [*aside:*] So must I teach myself to call him, then,
             Though in these many hours of fantasy
             He was call'd Calvin in our married life.
             [*To Marty:*] 'Tis well to meet thee, Calvin—
                                           Marty Klein. 45
                          [She sits next to him on the bed.
             Is it agreeable, that I sit here?
MARTY   O fine, 'tis fine. 'Tis well and fine. Fine well.
LORRAINE   The bruise upon thy head is passing large . . .
                          *[Lorraine reaches for Marty, who moves
                              backward and falls off the bed.*
STELLA   [*offstage:*] Lorraine, art thou up there?
LORRAINE   —My mother, fie!
             Put on thy denim pantaloons anon,   50
             And join my fam'ly at the supper table!
                          [Marty puts on his pants.
MARTY   This situation goes from bad to worse:
             My mother, now a youth, doth gaze on me
             As if she were a doe and I the buck!

                    Enter STELLA BAINES.

STELLA   Young Marty, welcome to our humble home.   55
             Pray, how long hath thy ship been in the port?
MARTY   Excuse me, for thy question is unclear.
STELLA   I guess'd thou wert a sailor by thy clothes—
             'Tis wherefore thou dost sport a life preserver.
MARTY   The Coast Guard, truly. Semper paratus.   60

They walk into the family room.
Enter SAM, MILTON, SALLY, TOBY, *and* JOEY BAINES,
preparing for dinner. SAM *attempts to make a television work.*

STELLA   Sam, meet the young man thou didst nearly slay.
                He fareth well, the gods above be thank'd.

SAM   Why wert thou in the middle of the street?
                A lad thine age.

STELLA   —O, pay to him no heed.
                The man is in a bitter mood tonight.   65
                Now, Sam, quit tampering with that machine—
                For supper is upon us. Marty, dear,
                Thou know'st Lorraine, meet also all her kin:
                There's Milton, Sally, Toby, and—just there,
                Inside the playpen—little baby Joey.   70

MARTY   [*aside, to Joey:*] Thou art mine uncle, Jailbird Joey, eh?
                Methinks thou shouldst become accustom'd to
                The bars of this, thy playpen, toddling knave!

STELLA   Young Joey loveth being in his pen
                And cries whenever he is taken out.   75
                We, therefore, leave him constantly inside,
                For what, methinks, could be the long-term harm?
                And now, to eat. Dost thou like meatloaf, Marty?

MARTY   Indeed, yet I should—

LORRAINE   —Marty, sit thou here.
                [*Lorraine pushes a chair behind Marty, into*
                                              which he falls.

STELLA   Sam, I shall not repeat myself again—   80
                Come hither now, stop playing with th'machine.
                Be thou a charming host and take thy seat.

SAM   Ha, ha! The matter is resolv'd at last—

The television worketh, by my wit.
We shall watch Jackie Gleason as we eat.   85

LORRAINE 'Tis our first television, verily—
My father hath acquir'd the thing today.
Hast thou a television, too, sweet Marty?

MARTY Of course, as thou shouldst know—we two possess.

MILTON Two, truly? Zounds, thou must be wondrous rich.   80

STELLA O, Milton, nay, the youth dost jest with thee,
For no one hath two television sets.
'Twould be a luxury beyond belief,
An excess past imagination's bounds.

MARTY This program is familiar unto me—   85
I watch'd it once before; a classic 'tis.
Herein Ralph dresses as an alien,
"Bang, zoom!" he doth exclaim, like one from space.

MILTON What meanest thou hast watch'd the show ere now?
'Tis new, and not from some past wonder year.   90

MARTY Indeed, for thee. I spied it on a rerun.

MILTON What means this word, this rerun?

MARTY   —Thou shalt learn.

STELLA Thou seemest so familiar to mine eyes.
Know I thy mother?

MARTY   —Likely, very likely.

STELLA Then should I call her soon, that she may have   95
No cause to worry o'er thy whereabouts.

MARTY Thou canst not, mayst not, shalt not—er, I mean—
What I should say is no one is at home.

STELLA Hmm.

MARTY   —Not yet.

STELLA   —Hmm.

MARTY [aside:]   —Another subject, quickly.

	[*to all*:] Say, do ye ken the lane called Riverside? 100
SAM	'Tis on the other end of our fair town,
	One block past Maple, on the eastern side.
MARTY	Did I hear right? One block past Maple, yea?
	'Tis nam'd for John F. Kennedy, is't not?
SAM	By all that is in heaven or in hell, 105
	Tell me: who is this John F. Kennedy?
LORRAINE	O Mother, if 'tis true that Marty's parents
	Are trav'ling now, should he not spend the night?
	'Tis but our Christian duty, is it not?
	To show our hospitality to strangers, 110
	And mayhap entertain the angels thus?
	'Tis certain Father nearly kill'd him when
	He struck him with our wagon earlier.
STELLA	Indeed, Lorraine doth speak the truth, young Marty.
	Belike thou should remain here for a night, 115
	Watch'd over by the Baineses and their bairns.
	Thy life is our responsibility.
MARTY	I do not know if 'tis a good idea . . .
LORRAINE	He shall sleep in my room, e'en in my bed,
	His tender cheek upon my pillow, yea, 120
	His dreams caught in the ether with mine own,
	And dancing merrily toward our future.

[Lorraine grasps Marty's knee
under the dinner table.

MARTY	Alas, 'tis time to flee, to fly, to flow.
	'Twas wonderful to meet ye, thank you all.
	You were a gracious, gen'rous family, 125
	And later I shall see ye once again.
	Much later, far, far later, by my troth.

[Exit Marty.

STELLA   A strange young man, indeed. Aye, passing strange.
SAM   An idiot, a folly-fallen rogue.
              It is his upbringing, I have no doubt.   130
              His errant parents, though I know them not,
              May also be describ'd as idiots.
              Lorraine, I bid thee hear thy father's words:
              An thou hast simple children such as he,
              Be sure I shall disown thee presently.   135

                                                          [*Exeunt.*

SCENE 2

At Doc Brown's house and just outside Hill Valley.

Enter MARTY MCFLY. *The DeLorean is aside,*
outside of town, beneath some bushes.

MARTY   Here am I: sixteen forty Riverside—
              Though known to me as John F. Kennedy—
              Wherein I should find Doc and make some sense
              Of all that I have seen since I arriv'd.
              Already have I witness'd things that I   5
              Would never have believ'd, e'en yesterday.
              My father and my mother both so young,
              And fill'd with life and vigor as I ne'er
              Have seen, their future still in front of them.
              Doc shall know how to get me hence from here,   10
              And take me once more to my rightful home.

Behold this house, how glorious and tall,
A mansion such as Doc could ne'er afford.
This must be that which once did catch afire,
Yet have I come before the match is struck. 15
I'll knock upon the heavy wooden door—
Ne'er was a knock so vital to my life.

He knocks. Enter DOCTOR EMMETT BROWN
at the door, wearing a contraption on his head.

  Doc, is it thee?
DOC   —Speak not a word, I pray.
         [They enter the house.
  Come thou inside, yet tell me not thy name,
  Nor aught about thy life or thine intent. 20
MARTY Doc, I—
DOC   —Nay, quiet! Tell me nothing, lad!
MARTY 'Tis me, 'tis Marty. Thou must help me, Doc.
DOC Tut, tut! Say naught, whilst I experiment.
    [Doc affixes a large sensor to Marty's forehead.
  Thy thoughts I'll read an 'twere a tome of tales,
  As plain as Homer's texts and Aesop's fables. 25
  Thou comest from a mighty distance.
MARTY   —Yea!
DOC Hush, do not tell—for I may clearly read.
  Thou comest in the hope that I, from thee,
  Shall buy a regular subscription to
  The *Sat'rday Evening Post*! 'Tis true?
MARTY   —Nay, Doc. 30
DOC Art thou a politician, thus to speak
  When none would wish to hear thee? Cease thy prattle.

I'll read thy book again, and know its plot:
Thou wouldst receive, from me, donations for
The Coast Guard Youth Auxiliary. Aye?   35
       [Marty pulls the sensor from his forehead.

MARTY   Doc, hear me: I have from the future come.
Within a time machine of thine invention
Have I come hither—nineteen fifty-five.
Thy help I do require, to take me back
Unto mine own time—nineteen eighty-five.   40

DOC   My God above—dost thou know what this means?
The import of thy words unto my work?
The finding thou hast here put on display?
It means this damn contraption worketh not!

MARTY   Doc, thou must help, though thou believ'st me not.   45
Thou art the only one who knowledge hath
Of how this time machine of thine doth work!

DOC   A time machine? I've not invented such.

MARTY   I'll prove it to thee, Doc. Behold this card:
My license wherewith I may drive a car—   50
It doth expire in nineteen eighty-seven.
See thou my birthday—I am not yet born!
This picture, too, see and believe, old friend:
My brother and my sister and myself.
The shirt she weareth tells the tale entire—   55
It readeth "Class of nineteen eighty-four."

DOC   'Tis mediocre photographic fak'ry,
A child would do a better job than this
Most shoddy work by amateurish hand.
Thy brother's hair is cut off from the rest.   60

MARTY   I tell thee nothing but the honest truth.
Thou must believe, or find me a grave man.

DOC   Pray tell me, then, thou future lad—who is
            The president of these United States
            Where thou com'st from: thy nineteen eighty-five?   65

MARTY   'Tis Ronald Reagan.

DOC   —He? The actor? Ha!
            Is Jerry Lewis, then, vice president?
            Jane Wyman, I suppose, is our first lady?
            Jack Benny, secretary of the treas'ry?
            Shall jesters, then, become our senators?   70
            Shall wrestling men become our governors?
            Shall businessmen turn into heads of state?
                                [*Doc begins to leave.*

MARTY   What, ho! Stay, Doc! I bid thee, wait and hear.

DOC   Good even—of thy jests I've had enow.
            Farewell, thou future lad, I shall no more.   75
                [*Doc shuts a door on Marty. Marty talks to him*
                                through the door.

MARTY   Nay, Doc, I yet may prove I speak the truth.
            The bruise thou hast, upon thy head of white,
            I know whence it hath come, yea, and wherefore;
            Thou didst unfold to me the tale entire.
            Upon the precipice of thy commode   80
            Thou stood'st, intent to fix a timepiece there.
            Thou fell'st and knock'dst thy head upon the sink.
            Then did a picture come into thy mind:
            Thy miracle, the flux capacitor,
            Which maketh possible time travel. Truly,   85
            Believ'd I not before, yet now I do.
                                [*Doc opens the door.*

DOC   Thy words, each one a wonder, do convince—
            However strange, I see thou speakest true.

MARTY   O blessèd change—thou hadst me worried so.
                  [They move to the hidden DeLorean.
      I hid the time machine outside the town.   90
      Something there is that doesn't love a starter—
      Therefore, beneath a bramble it doth lie
      Until it can be made to drive once more.

DOC   This strange contraption hath a car's appearance,
      Yet like no automobile I've e'er seen.   95
      Once I did fall, this morning, I drew this.
              [Doc pulls out a sketch of the flux capacitor.

MARTY   The flux capacitor—I know it well.
      Behold, my friend, the work of thirty years,
      As I exhibit how a simple sketch
      Hast, by thy hand, become reality.   100

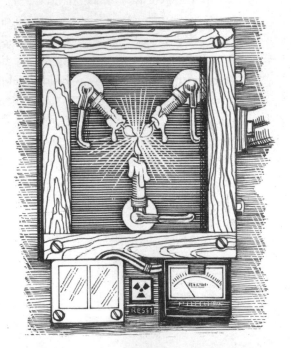

                                    [Marty opens the door and
                                    turns on the flux capacitor.

DOC   It worketh! O, it worketh—mark the day
             I finally invented aught that worketh!

MARTY   Most certain 'tis it worketh. That I stand
             In nineteen fifty-five is ample proof.
             Thou couldst bet bottom dollar it is so.   105

DOC   Let us sneak this unto my lab'ratory.
             We shall return thee home, this do I vow!
                     [They push the DeLorean back to Doc's house.

MARTY   The night we sent me hither, to this time,
             We made a record of th'experiment.
             This video I shall connect unto   110
             Thy television, that thou mayst behold.
                     [Marty connects the camera to the television.
             Come now, and thou shalt see what we have done.

The video begins playing. DOC *from the future speaks in the video.*

DOC   'Tis I! Observe how old I have become.
VIDEO DOC   Friends, makers, countrymen, lend me your ears—
             My name ye know: 'tis Doctor Emmett Brown.   115
             I stand upon the stony parking lot
             Of Twin Pines Mall, Hill Valley, California.

DOC   Thanks be to God I still have all my hair,
             Yet what are these strange garments I am wearing?

MARTY   Array'd art thou in radiation suit.   120

DOC   A radiation suit? Of course, of course!
             From all the fallout of atomic war—
             Methought it would be so; I see it is,
             For never was there peacetime made to last.

| | Meanwhile, this small contraption doth amaze— | 125 |

Meanwhile, this small contraption doth amaze—   125
A handheld television studio,
With which one may record whate'er transpires.
No wonder 'tis, thy president was once
An actor, with his name known through the Globe;
His visage and comportment must be pleasing   130
Unto a television audience.

MARTY   I have advanc'd the tape unto the part
That I would have thee see, Doc. Vital 'tis.

VIDEO DOC Nay, nay, the splendid craft's electrical—
Yet it requires a nuclear reaction   135
To generate the mighty current of
The one point twenty-one in gigawatts—

DOC   What did I say? I prithee, play it back.

[Marty rewinds the tape.

VIDEO DOC Nay, nay, the splendid craft's electrical—
Yet it requires a nuclear reaction   140
To generate the mighty current of
The one point twenty-one in gigawatts
Of pow'r electrical that I do need.

DOC   Fie! One point twenty-one in gigawatts!
Foh! Gigawatts of one point twenty-one!   145
Great Scott! What have I done? How can it be?

MARTY   Doc, what in hell's name is a gigawatt?

DOC   How could I be so careless, so unthinking?
O, one point twenty-one in gigawatts.

[Doc picks up a picture of Thomas Edison.

Tom—friend, companion, and inventor wise—   150
How shall I generate this awesome pow'r?
Not even thee—in all thy harsh debates
With Tesla, as your two most brilliant minds

	Did wrestle with these matters most electric—	
	Conceive of such a great and stagg'ring sum	155
	As one point twenty-one in gigawatts.	
	It cannot be accomplish'd, can it? Nay!	
MARTY	'Tis simple, Doc, and I shall tell thee how,	
	As thou in thirty years wilt tell it me:	
	We need no more than some plutonium.	160
DOC	Ha! In thy nineteen eighty-five, perchance,	
	Plutonium is found in ev'ry market,	
	Upon the shelves with cheese or eggs or milk,	
	As simple in the buying as a pear	
	Or onions for a picknick at the park.	165
	In nineteen fifty-five, however, 'tis	
	Far harder to obtain plutonium.	
	With my regrets, good Marty, I'll explain:	
	Thou shalt be bound unto this present time,	
	Canst never leave as long as thou shalt live.	170
MARTY	Canst never leave—O, speak thou not these words!	
	I must return, and not be here confin'd.	
	A life I have in nineteen eighty-five.	
	Moreover, there's my lass, my Jennifer,	
	Who, like the loyal, true Penelope,	175
	Will be there waiting for me.	
DOC	—Is she fair?	
MARTY	Her beauty is beyond compare to me	
	And, whether 'tis by luck or miracle,	
	She loveth me with whole and eager heart.	
	Look thou upon this note that she hath writ,	180
	Wherein she doth proclaim her love for me.	
	This simple paper verifies my claims.	
DOC	Incomprehensible this matter is.	

MARTY   Pray, say not so: thou art mine only hope.

DOC   I'm sorry, Marty, but the only source   185
          That can such massive electricity
          Produce—to reach the pow'rful magnitude,
          E'en one point twenty-one in gigawatts—
          Of which I know—is from a lightning bolt.

MARTY   What hast thou said? Again?

DOC   —A lightning bolt.   190
          Unfortunately, 'tis impossible,
          Unless thou can communicate with Zeus,
          Ask him to lend to thee his flaming rods,
          And have the gods look kindly on thy quest.
          The matter hopeless is! For none do know   195
          The when or where a lightning bolt shall strike.

MARTY   None save one who hath from the future come!
          We knoweth well, behold this pamphlet here,
          Which 'pon the back my Jennifer did write.

                    [Marty hands the pamphlet to Doc.

DOC   Our town's clock tower, struck by lightning, eh?   200
          And 'twill be soon—the time doth come apace.
          Thou hast the answer, Marty, this is it!
          This pamphlet doth report a lightning bolt
          Shall strike the large clock tower on the stroke
          Of ten oh four at night on Saturday—   205
          This coming Saturday, by happenstance!
          If we, mayhap, can harness all the pow'r
          That cometh from the lightning's mighty bolt,
          Direct it to the flux capacitor,
          And do so at the perfect instant, too,   210
          Belike the plan shall work, and send thee home.
          Upon the night of Saturday the next,

	We'll send thee back to the future, forsooth!
MARTY	A-ha! 'Tis well, and Saturday sufficeth!

We'll send thee back to the future, forsooth!

MARTY   A-ha! 'Tis well, and Saturday sufficeth!
A fortnight's half in nineteen fifty-five   215
Shall be like a vacation for my soul.
Thou canst show me Hill Valley of the past,
I'll hang about and lunch at Lou's Café.

DOC   Nay, Marty, nay, this must not—cannot—be.
There is no question of thy living life   220
An 'twere a holiday that thou enjoy'st.
Thou must remain herein, within this house,
And neither see nor talk with anyone.
Aught thou shalt do—the smallest action ta'en—
May lead to repercussions serious.   225
'Tis like the fable thou hast surely heard:
Recall the one who travell'd back in time,
And did no more than crush a butterfly—
Yet when he did return unto his time,
All had been chang'd by his most careless act,   230
His future was unwittingly transform'd.
Time builds on time as if 'twere dominos—
When one doth fall, the others fall thereafter,
The sequence vital. When 'tis modified,
The future is unrecognizable.   235
Say, dost thou comprehend these crucial words?

MARTY   [aside:] Alas, methinks Doc's warning is too late.
[To Doc:] Indeed, 'tis plain. My thanks for thy concern.

DOC   O Marty, hast thou interaction had
With anybody else, besides myself?   240

MARTY   'Tis possible my parents I have seen,
Perhaps some unexpected scenes withal.

DOC   Great Scott! I prithee, let me see again

The photograph of thou and siblings two.

                [Marty hands Doc the photograph.

'Tis as I fear'd—my theory hath been prov'n.   245

Behold thy brother, headless like the horseman.

MARTY   Completely gone, like it had been eras'd.

DOC   Not simply from the photograph gone hence—

Deleted utterly, from all existence.

Young Marty, in thy brief encounters here   250

Thou hast fall'n in a situation grave.

Whate'er hath happen'd shall we two negate—

Thine actions we'll undo or be undone.

Thou, somehow, hast unspun the knit of Fate,

And sewn new patterns that shall work thee woe.   255

Already dost the thread work on thy brother;

More like a noose unto his missing head.
Upon the morrow, let our work begin;
Ne'er hath a challenge made Doc Brown afeard.
We shall unto the school, where we two shall   260
Retie this knot betwixt thy mom and dad.
Thy future time, therefore, thou mayst still claim—
Familiar, unaffected, still the same.

[Exeunt.

SCENE 3

At Hill Valley High School.

Enter MARTY MCFLY *and* DOC BROWN.

MARTY   The school doth look so tidy, fresh, and new,
          As though a dignitary were expected.
DOC   Remember, if my theory is correct,
          Thou hast, by chance, in some way interfer'd
          At the first meeting of thy parents two.   5
          If they meet not, they shall not fall in love,
          If they fall not in love, they shall not marry,
          If they do marry not, they'll have no offspring,
          And if they have no offspring, Marty, then
          I fear for thee—what may on thee befall.   10
          Methinks 'tis why thine older brother Dave
          Is disappearing from the photograph.
          Thine older sister follows him in time;

	Unless thou canst repair the damage done,	
	'Twill be thy fate as well, to disappear.	15
MARTY	So heavy is this matter, by my troth.	
DOC	Nay, Marty, weight hath naught to do withal.	

Enter GEORGE McFLY *and other* HIGH SCHOOL STUDENTS.
Enter LORRAINE BAINES *aside, with her* FRIENDS.

	The students come! Which pupil is thy father?	
MARTY	Just there, assaulted by a band of boys.	
	[Some boys kick George as he walks down the hall with a KICK ME *sign upon his back.*	
GEORGE	Enow, enow, ha ha, your jests are o'er.	20
	Ye are so funny and mature as well.	
MARTY	[*aside:*] How it doth pain me, seeing Father thus.	
	Some brute hath written "kick me" on a sign,	
	Affix'd it to my father's waiting back,	
	And now the cowards render him his due.	25
	O Father, was it ever thus for thee?	
DOC	Mayhap thou wert adopted, possibly?	
GEORGE	[*to the boys:*] A jest indeed, and full of wit and mirth.	
	Your nasty kicks hath made me drop my books.	
	Which one of ye shall pick them up?	
	[Exeunt boys.	

Enter SIR STRICKLAND.

STRICK.	—McFly!	30
MARTY	By Jove, Sir Strickland! Thirty years unchang'd—	
	Hath this mean man ne'er had a wisp of hair?	
	Belike his constant baldness turn'd him sour!	

STRICK.	Take care, McFly, and shipshape make thyself—
	Thou art a slacker and a laggard, too. 35
	Wouldst thou be thus abus'd thy life entire?
GEORGE	Nay.
	[Exit Sir Strickland in disgust.
DOC	—Wherefore did thy mother give him notice?
	How lookèd she with favor on this imp?
MARTY	I know not, Doc. She says she pitied him
	Because her father struck him with their car. 40
	Aye, there's the rub—he struck not George, but me.
DOC	'Tis known in scientific circles as
	The Florence Nightingale effect, indeed:
	To fall in love with one for whom one helps.
	It happens also in our hospitals, 45
	When nurses with their patients are enamor'd.
	Now to thy work, good lad, undoing that
	Which thou mistakenly hast done before.
	[Marty approaches George and
	helps him pick up his books.
MARTY	George, friend and comrade mine, how hast thou been?
	I nearly ev'rywhere have search'd for thee. 50
	Dost thou remember me, the person who
	Hath rescued thee from harm not long ago?
GEORGE	Indeed.
MARTY	—Good! There is someone thou
	shouldst meet.
	[Marty guides George over to
	Lorraine and her friends.
	Lorraine, hello!
LORRAINE	—O, Calvin! Thou art here.
	Thou whom I fear'd I'd never see again. 55

MARTY   Pray, let me introduce thee to my friend—
             A lad of some renown, and handsome, too,
             A lord to a lord, a man to a man,
             Stuff'd with all honorable virtues, yea,
             A person excellent—'tis George McFly.   60

GEORGE   The pleasure of the meeting is mine own.

LORRAINE   [*to Marty, ignoring George:*] How is thy precious,
                                          pitiable pate?
                                    [*Exit George in dismay.*

MARTY   'Tis fine, 'tis well.

LORRAINE   —So worried have I been,
             Since thou did wander hence the other night.
             Pray tell me, art thou well? For if thou'rt not,   65
             I shall be sadder than the day is long.

MARTY   Be not afraid, for I am well, indeed.
                                    [*The school bell rings.*

LORRAINE   Alas, I'm bound to fly to my next class.
             I must see thee again. [*To her friends:*] See what I said?
             Is he not captain of a mighty ship?   70
             The pilot of a dreamboat in th'extreme!
                                    [*Exeunt all but Marty and Doc.*

MARTY   How shall I play these cards, Doc, for the girl
             Hath hardly look'd in his direction. See?

DOC   The situation's worse than I had thought—
             The odds are stack'd against our weaker hand.   75
             Apparently, this queen would take the jack,
             Instead of the true king who suits her best.
             Thy mother is infatuated with
             Her son—e'en thee!—as if we were the Greeks,
             And you an Oedipus to her Jocasta.   80

MARTY   What? Wait one moment, Doc. What didst thou say?

	Dost say my mother burneth hot for me?
DOC	Precisely thus.
MARTY	—'Tis heavy, by my troth.
DOC	There is the word, which thou dost use again:

'Tis heavy, all is heavy unto thee.   85
Why hath the future so much heaviness?
Hath aught disrupted something in the Earth,
Affecting its own pull of gravity?

MARTY   What? Is it ever only science with thee?
DOC   The only way those Homo sapiens   90
Shall be convinc'd to mate with one another,
Is to get them together, by themselves.
Thy mother and thy father, therefore, must
Have interaction in a social space—

MARTY   A date, in layman's terms? Such dost thou mean?   95
DOC   Forsooth!
MARTY   —Yet I have no idea, for what
Do children of the nineteen fifties do?
DOC   They are thy parents—or shall one day be—
Thou must know aught about their pref'rences.
What are their common interests and likes?   100
How do they pass their many hours together?

MARTY   Naught that doth come to mind.
                           [Doc notices a sign on the wall.
DOC   —Behold this sign!
A rhythmic ceremon'al ritual
Approacheth, on our vital Saturday.
MARTY   Th'Enchantment 'Neath the Sea dance, Doc, of
                                   course! 105
The memory comes swiftly to my mind—
It is their fate together to attend,

Wherein the lovers shall their first kiss share.

DOC   The plan is seal'd, the wheels are set in motion.

Stick to thy father an 'twere glue to wood.   110

No more shall we be led by happenstance—

Make certain that he takes her to the dance!

[Exeunt.

SCENE 4

In the Hill Valley High School cafeteria.

Enter GEORGE MCFLY, *seated alone at a table. Enter other*
STUDENTS *including* LORRAINE BAINES *aside, with her* FRIENDS.

GEORGE   Alone, as usual—another lunch

With only pen and paper at my side,

Mine only friends with which to spend my time.

I shall immerse myself in other worlds,

Attempt to be like those who go before—   5

Ray Bradbury, the author of my heart,

Whose books do burn like fire within my hands.

Or Isaac Asimov, who pictures what

A future most robotic shall be like.

There's Robert Heinlein, taking us away   10

To other worlds where aliens await.

I follow in their footsteps carefully,

My footprints paling by comparison.

Yet I must write. If I say I shall not,

The words are in my heart an 'twere a fire,   15
A vast inferno shut up in my bones.
I weary of the holding it inside;
Indeed, I cannot—I am doom'd to write.

Enter MARTY MCFLY.

MARTY   George, friend. Dost thou recall the lass Lorraine,
               Whom I did introduce to thee of late?   20
GEORGE   [*aside:*] The lady is not soon forgotten, nay.
MARTY   What dost thou write?
GEORGE   —'Tis stories, fables, myths.
               A science-fiction tale of visitors
               Who come to Earth from other brave new worlds.
MARTY   [*aside:*] My father, he the author? History   25
               Containeth more surprises than methought.
               [*To George:*] 'Tis true? Thou speakest verily, my friend?
               I did not know thou wert a writer, George,
               Or had a shred of creativity.
               Wouldst let me read?
GEORGE   —Nay, ne'er. Apologies,   30
               It is my wont to never share my tales.
MARTY   Yet wherefore not? Why shouldst thou hide thy gift?
GEORGE   If I should let a reader see my tale—
               My secret visions and my fantasies—
               Pretending it is worthy of their time   35
               Or that they might enjoy the world I build,
               Such venture would be dangerous, indeed.
               To write or to create is to be brave,
               Each work of art an act of courage, too;
               Releasing it to critics is too far.   40

Say that, on reading it, they said, "A-ha!
You are no writer, nay, you are a fraud!
No publisher will ever look on this,
Declare it finely writ, and print the drivel.
Relinquish all thy dreams, you worthless rogue,   45
Or you shall surely be a laughingstock!"
Methinks the harsh rejection would destroy me,
Eviscerated by opinion's blade.

MARTY   [*aside:*] His writing and my music are the same—
The art for which we suffer, fear, and doubt.   50
[*To George:*] Yet George, what of Lorraine? She liketh
                                                        thee,
And told me I should tell thee to ask her
To take her to th'Enchantment 'Neath the Sea.

GEORGE   Yea, verily?

MARTY   —I would not lie to thee.
'Tis simple—thither go and ask the lass.   55

GEORGE   E'en here? Within the cafeteria?
What if she answer'd nay? What then befalls?
I could not take such sharp humiliation.

Enter BIFF TANNEN, *with* SKINHEAD, 3-D, *and* MATCH,
crossing to LORRAINE.

Besides, another reason fills mine eyes;
Belike she'd gladly go with someone else.   60

MARTY   Whom dost thou mean?

GEORGE   —E'en Biff, 'tis plain. Behold.

BIFF   [*to Lorraine:*] Be not so timid, lass. Thou likest me,
And wantest Biff to give himself to thee.

LORRAINE   Thy mouth be shut! I am not thus inclin'd.

                                              [She slaps him.
BIFF   Belike thou art, but dost not know it yet.   65
LORRAINE   Thy filthy hands, like claws, remove from me!
                    [Marty approaches then and grabs Biff.
MARTY   An thou hast ears—as thou most plainly dost—
              Thou must have heard the lass. Take heed, or else—
              She said thy filthy hands remove from her!
              [Aside:] Now that he stands, how large he looms o'er
                                                        me! 70
BIFF   What is it unto thee, thou arse-like pate?
              Thou hast been begging for some fisticuffs
              Since first we met. Now shalt thou get thy wish.

              They nearly fight. Enter SIR STRICKLAND.

STRICK.   I have no need to raise my voice to make
              My presence heard. 'Tis good to be the king.   75
BIFF   *[aside, to Marty:]* I shall—because thou to our school
                                                   art new—
              Grant thee, this once, a merciful reprieve.
              Now make thou like a tree, and thither flee.
                         [Exeunt all save Marty and George.
MARTY   George, hear me, please.
GEORGE   —Why dost thou follow me?
MARTY   Pray, listen, George, and hear my truth again: 80
              If thou ask'st not Lorraine unto the dance,
              I shall regret thy failure all my days.
GEORGE   Nay, all occasions do inform against me
              And tell me I may not this dance attend.
              For if I do, I'll miss my fav'rite show,   85
              E'en *Science Fiction Theatre.* Dost hear?

MARTY   Yet, George, Lorraine desires to go with thee.
             Show her some pity, else thou break'st her heart.

GEORGE   Thou dost not heed my words in anywise:
             I'm not prepar'd to ask Lorraine to go   90
             To the Enchantment 'Neath the Sea dance, nay,
             And neither thou nor any on this planet
             Could change my mind. 'Tis fix'd. 'Tis settl'd. Nay.
                                            [Exit George.

MARTY   This conversation hath not gone my way,
             And I am getting desp'rate, for behold: 95
             The picture of my siblings grows more bleak,
             My brother fully disappear'd except
             The bottoms of his legs—O, tragic Dave,
             Become a pair of calves and heels and feet.
             Next shall kind Linda disappear as well,   100
             Then I shall go—be truly gone, indeed.
             Some new solution I must undertake.
             The words George spake ring gently on mine ears—
             These: "Neither thou nor any on this planet
             Could change my mind." Belike this dreamer
                                            George— 105
             Who writeth science fiction and doth keep
             His head too often out among the spheres—
             Would answer better to another call.
             If he wants *Science Fiction Theatre*,
             I shall deliver thus unto his home,   110
             Before his face, and ringing in his ears.
             No visitor from Earth shall make George brave;
             Thus space shall come to him, my life to save.
                                            [Exit.

SCENE 5

In the town of Hill Valley.

Enter GEORGE McFLY.

GEORGE Ay me, for pity! What a dream was here!
 In th'middle of the night, whilst I did sleep,
 Abed and peaceful, naught disturbing me,
 I heard a sudden shrieking in mine ears.
 'Twas like a horrible, unearthly sound,   5
 More frightful than I thought was possible.
 I woke upon the instant and beheld
 A creature garb'd in yellow, with a mask
 That captur'd ev'ry terror in my brain
 As if it read my worried, anxious mind   10
 And did display its worst imaginings.
 Its visage was the perfect likeness of
 The aliens, which I had lately seen
 Within *Fantastic Story Magazine.*
 "Who are you?" I did ask, with fear and trem'bling. 15
 As if I had offended or upset it,
 It pointed its device toward my head
 And suddenly the noise did screech again,
 My head fill'd with the pounding, awful sound.
 At last it spoke: "Be silent, earthling weak. 20
 Darth Vader am I call'd, of strength and pow'r,
 An extrat'rrestrial from Vulcan come."
 It made a sign then, with its clawlike hand,
 Which hypnotiz'd me by some sorcery,

And bent my mind, that I might do its will.   25
The strange and unrelenting force it us'd
Surrounded me, and shall be with me always.
I'll not live long and prosper if I should
Ignore the message it hath brought to me.

Enter MARTY MCFLY.

A-ha! Good Marty, I must tell him all,   30
For he hath been mine only friend of late.
Ho, Marty!
MARTY   —George, why comest thou in haste?
Thou wert not there in school. Where hast thou been?
How hast thou spent the first hours of the day?
GEORGE   I slept too long, and I shall tell thee why.   35
Yet first, I shall confess: I need thy help.
Lorraine I must invite unto the dance,
Yet do not have the wisdom or the words
To see it through.
MARTY   —Be patient, I shall help.
She is just yonder, there in Lou's Café.   40
What was the cause of this most sudden change?
For yesterday, thou wert of rigid mind,
As constant as the northern star, indeed.
GEORGE   The tale I'll tell, though thou mayst not believe:
Last night hath come Darth Vader to my house   45
From planet Vulcan. He hath order'd me
To take Lorraine unto this weekend's dance
Or he would swiftly melt my guiltless brain.
MARTY   Thy tale of melting brains we'll not divulge,
For though I do believe, it may sound strange   50

	To others less supportive than myself.
GEORGE	In sooth, I would not tell another soul.

> *[They approach Lou's Café.*

MARTY	There, just inside, she waiteth for thee, George.
	Be bold, walk in, and make thine invitation.
GEORGE	Yet I have not the words to make it so. 55
MARTY	Say anything that cometh to thy mind—
	The world is full of guys. Be thou a man.
	Whatever is most natural to thee,
	Which springeth first unto thy fertile mind.
GEORGE	'Tis winter in my brain, for nothing comes. 60
MARTY	By Jove, it is a wonder I was born!
GEORGE	What?
MARTY	—Nothing, nothing, nay. Pray, tell her this:
	Say fate hath knit thy twofold souls as one,
	And destiny hath brought thee both together.

> *[George pulls out a pencil and paper.*

	Speak softly to her tender ears that she 65
	Hath beauty more than any other girl—
	That thou couldst search the world entire in vain
	And ne'er wouldst find her match upon the Earth.
	Such words fall gently on romantic ears.
	Art thou turn'd scribe, that thou wouldst write this
	down? 70
GEORGE	Thou art well-vers'd in love's confusing syntax—
	The Cyrano unto my Neuvillette.
MARTY	The time hath come. Gird up thy loins and speak.

They walk into Lou's Café.

Enter LOU CARUTHERS, GOLDIE WILSON, LORRAINE BAINES *with her*
FRIENDS, *and many other* YOUTH OF HILL VALLEY.

GEORGE   Lou, give me milk—and make it chocolate!
                              [A glass slides down the bar
                              to George, who drinks deeply.
             [*Aside:*] Dutch courage will give me the strength I
                                                        need— 75
             Dutch chocolate hath ne'er led me astray.
             [*To Lorraine:*] Lorraine, my density has brought me
                                                        here.

LORRAINE   Excuse me?
GEORGE   —Pardon, this I meant to say . . .
LORRAINE   Do I not know thee somehow? Tell me true.
GEORGE   Indeed, dear lass, my name is George McFly!   80
             I am thy density . . . er, destiny.
             There ne'er was one so dense for thee as I,
             Fill'd so completely with a love as mine
             And destin'd, thereupon, for dense romance.

             Enter BIFF TANNEN, SKINHEAD, 3-D,
                and MATCH, *aside.*

LORRAINE   Thy words are like a puzzle for the ear,   85
             Which, kindly spoken, stupefy the mind.
             So sweet thou art, if somewhat mystifying.
BIFF   McFly!
MARTY   [*aside:*] —Fie, hatred comes to hinder love,
             As if the minotaur held Cupid's bow.
BIFF   Methought I said thou ne'er shouldst hither come, 90
             Yet thou hast giv'n no heed to warnings fair.
             This time, thy grave mistake shall have a cost—
             Shall it be coin or flesh? We'll see anon.
             How many ducats dost thou carry, hmm?

GEORGE   How much dost thou desire, O massive Biff?   95
                Whate'er thou wishest shall be my command.
                                    [Biff approaches George
                                    and is tripped by Marty.

MARTY   [aside:] He falls, yet what shall now on me befall?
                            [Biff rises, towering over Marty.

BIFF   Thou puny, craven, dismal-dreaming imp!
                This is the opportunity I've sought.
                Wilt thou take on the Biff? Now, feel my pow'r—   100

MARTY   Yet, Biff, what is that yon, outside the window?
                        [Biff looks and Marty hits him. Marty flees,
                        knocking over Skinhead, 3-D, and Match.

SKINHEAD   Alack!

3-D   —Undone by such a one?

MATCH   —We fall!

LORRAINE   'Tis Calvin Klein! By Jove, a perfect dream.
                            [The scene moves outside,
                            as Biff begins chasing after Marty
                                through Hill Valley.

MARTY   Too long I cannot relish victory;
                'Tis certain trouble follows me anon.   105
                Fly, feet, and bear me hence away from Biff,
                Before I face the terror of his wrath.
                From Lou's Café I flee to save myself,
                No more belike to darken these two doors.
                Across the street, I see my greatest hope—   110
                A boy doth hold a wooden scooter toy,
                Which, by a brief amendment, may suffice.
                The youth doth fuss at me, an 'twere I took
                His childhood whole e'en as I take his toy.
                Fear not, O lad; I'll render it again,   115

That thou once more may ride Hill Valley's roads.
First, though, to make the scooter fit for me—
Its top remov'd, it doth become a skateboard
Wherewith I shall defeat the coming threat.
"Thou brokest it," the whining schoolboy says,   120
Yet as I speed away his tone doth change:
"Look how he flieth on my scooterboard!"
Biff and his thugs pursue me on their feet—
They run across the courtyard while I'm bound
To use the sidewalk, an I would have wheels.   125
An old familiar trick I'll ply on them—
Hold fast unto this truck, and switch direction
Whilst their momentum carries them too far.
Too nearly miss'd—yea, far too close for comfort.
'Twas just in time (a simple, common phrase   130
That I, 'til recently, employ'd sans thought).
Now do I ride behind this helpful truck,
A subtle and unask'd-for hitchhiker,
As Biff and his three goons run to their car—
A vehicle I can no wise outrun.   135
Yet for a moment, Marty, let thyself
Enjoy the triumph of this fleeting moment.
See there, the youth who watch in Lou's Café,
Their mouths agape at my most daring flight.
I almost can their exclamations hear—   140
"What is it that the lad doth ride upon?"
"Methinks it is a wooden board, with wheels!"
Perhaps Lorraine, besotted by romance,
Declareth, "Lo, he is the stuff of dreams"—
A most disturbing thought, my mother thus.   145
Pray focus, for the rogues do come apace,

They shout like banshees, hungry for revenge,
Keen to protect their bully reputations,
Save face when challeng'd by a naughty sleight.
Biff piloteth the vehicle across   150
The courtyard, rolling o'er the town green's grass—
This foolish action is pure recklessness.
Mayhap I've underestimated them,
And did not sense the drama of the scene.
They follow close behind, approaching me;   155
A harmless scuffle twixt two high school lads
Hath turn'd into a chase most dangerous.
Although Biff's friends still cackle, rife with glee,
Biff hath another matter on his mind,
The heart of which shines forth from his dark eyes   160
An 'twere the reddish glow of hell's own heart.
Biff's ire transformeth to intent to kill.
The lads would brush my legs with their fast car—
I dodge aside, and now they strike the truck.
Another car is in the road ahead,   165
Which I shall knock, should I maintain my course.
Release the truck, yet still I roll too fast—
The newfound skateboard jumpeth in the air
As I attempt to keep my balance on't.
Too fast, too fast! I plunge toward a couple—   170
A man and woman, caught within my path.
We three collide—like ring around the rosie,
The ashes fly and then we all fall down.
I rise again, yet Biff is closer still—
No hope remains that I may him outpace.   175
The car doth strike me, pushing me along.
Biff's friends hurl bottles at me, like a target;

'Tis lucky each one is a dreadful aim.
Biff speaketh: "I shall ram the useless imp."
In front of me a dump truck comes in view—   180
Mine end is near, yet one maneuver may
Keep this from being Marty's tragic end.
I jump aboard the car, toward its rear,
My trusty skateboard following beneath.
Biff and his hoodlums look behind in awe;   185
They're dumbstruck, seeing not what they shall hit.
They shout, then strike the truck fill'd with manure,
Which falleth o'er them an 'twere graveyard dirt.
The owner of the scooter, which now smoketh,
Looks on with awe. Good lad, thou hast my thanks!   190
Yet now I'll leave, ere further trouble comes.

                      [Exit Marty.

FRIEND 1   [*to Lorraine:*] Whence cometh this amazing, handsome
                                lad?

If thou dost know, I prithee speak, Lorraine!
FRIEND 2   Where doth he live, or is he come from heav'n?
We must, in some way, learn whence he arriv'd.   195
LORRAINE I do not know, yet I shall learn anon.
The seed that first was planted in my home,
Wherein he first took root within my heart,
Hath budded into something greater yet—
A growth unstoppable, with mighty trunk,   200
A tree that with affection bursteth forth,
Each blossom telling of my love for him,
With branches reaching new heights ev'ry day.
I shall discover where this hardy stalk
Doth hath foundation, else my fondest hopes   205
Shall be chopp'd down with axe unkind and swift.

[Exeunt Lorraine and her friends.

BIFF   O, hear ye now the words I hereby swear:
I'll be reveng'd on him for this affair.

[Exeunt.

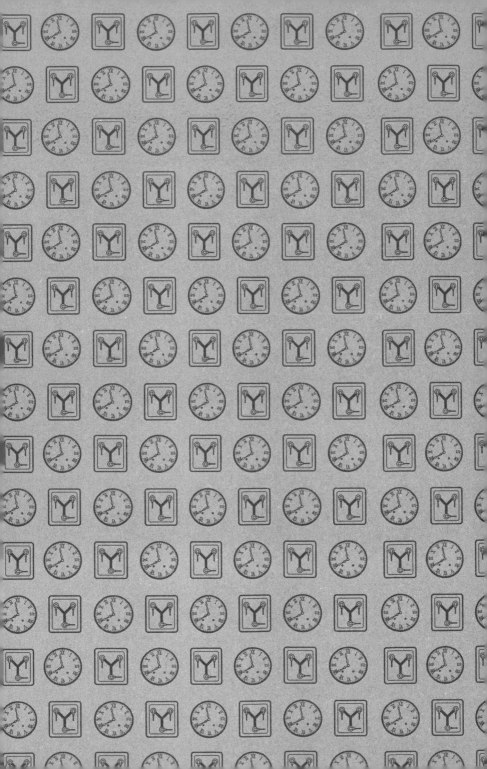

ACT IV

SCENE 1

At Doc Brown's house.

Enter DOCTOR EMMETT BROWN,
watching Marty's video on his television.

DOC   Reviewing this recording of the night
That Marty brought, from nineteen eighty-five,
I see myself caught under some distress,
Bewailing some unfortunate event,
And peradventure fearing for my life.   5
"My God. They found me. How, I do not know,
And yet 'tis clear they found me nonetheless."
Thus say I, then exclaim, "Run, Marty, run!"
What people have instill'd in me such fear?
From whom escape? I wonder what I mean.   10
This wondering, however—it must cease.
To know the future is too dangerous,
Too powerful a thing for mortal minds.
Methinks upon the tale of poor Cassandra.
She was a prophet—knowing what would come,   15
Yet she was doom'd to never be believ'd.
Her prophecies like noise fell on the ears
Of any who would hear her solemn words,
An 'twere a clanging symbol or a gong
To be ignor'd instead of being heeded.   20
The future is not ours to know, indeed,
For if we knew the future, we would live
To either bring it to fruition or

Mayhap to 'scape what it doth hold for us.
In either instance, we upset the Fates,   25
The fateful knitters of our future days,
The sisters who do hold the threads of life
And make determination o'er its length.
Sweet Clotho spins the fabric of our days,
While wise Lachesis doth allot the yarn.   30
To finish, Atropos doth cut the cord
As death doth shuffle off our mortal coil.
Let us not seek to know the future, nay;
'Tis kept by those more powerful than we.

       Enter MARTY MCFLY, *seeing* DOC.

MARTY   Doc?
DOC   —Marty! I did not hear thee arrive.   35
          A fascinating implement, this thing
          Which captures video to watch again.
MARTY   Pray, hear me, Doc. There's something I must say
          About the night we two produc'd that tape.
DOC   Nay, Marty, tell me naught. No man should know   40
          Too much about his final destiny.
MARTY   Thou dost not understand.
DOC   —I do, indeed.
          An I should know too much of what will come,
          Mine own existence could endanger'd be—
          Just as thou hast endanger'd thine. Dost see?   45
MARTY   Thou hast it right.
DOC   —Come, now, and see my plan,
          Wherewith I'll get thee hence unto thy home.

[Doc shows Marty a detailed
model of Hill Valley.

This crude and feeble model please forgive—
And let me, cipher to this great accompt,
On thine imaginary forces work. 50
Suppose within the cutouts of these walls
Are now confin'd Hill Valley's mighty town,
Whose high clock tower and the road below
Create the centerpiece of our design.
Piece out our imperfections with thy thoughts; 55
Into a thousand parts divide each inch,
And make imaginary structures there;
Think when we talk of buildings, that thou seest them
Printing their proud foundations in the earth;
For 'tis thy thoughts that now must deck our plans, 60
Though I had not the time to build to scale
Or make it truer by the splash of paint.

MARTY   'Tis well. It shall suffice.

DOC   —My gratitude.
We shall run cord of strength industrial
From here—the very height of our clock tower— 65
Below, suspending it just o'er the street,
Betwixt the lampposts that are fixèd there.
Meanwhile, the vehicle hath been enhanc'd
With this long pole and hook, which do connect
Directly to the flux capacitor. 70
Upon the instant I have calculated,
Thou shalt begin to drive the car from there—
A certain distance farther down the road—
Whilst steering it directly t'ward the cable
And making thine acceleration to 75

Precisely eighty-eight in miles per hour.
According to the pamphlet thou hast brought,
Upon the stroke of ten oh four at night,
Come Saturday this week, a lightning bolt
Shall strike the tower. Electricity   80
Will travel through the cable, bound to strike
The hook just as thou drivest it below.
The one point twenty-one in gigawatts
Shall, by this method, flow directly to
The flux capacitor. As a result,   85
Thou shalt return to nineteen eighty-five.
I prithee watch, as I do test the model.
Wind up the car, prepare it to release,
Whilst I make simulation of the lightning.

MARTY   [aside:] A man, a plan, a model—clever Doc!   90
DOC   Art thou prepar'd? Set thou the car. Let fly!

                        [Marty sets the car down,
                    and it rolls down the model road.
                    Doc sends electricity down the cable,
                        which strikes the car. Now aflame,
                            the car rolls off the model
                    and onto a sheet, setting it alight.

MARTY   Alack! Shall all my hopes go up in flame?
          This is a wicked portent, by my soul.
          But little confidence thou dost instill!
                        [Doc rushes to put out the fire.
DOC   A temporary setback to the model,   95
          Yet naught that shall keep us from this endeavor.
          Fear not, for I'll ensure the lightning strike
          Is well within our power to control.
          Thou, though, must work on more than lightning bolts,

And tame much greater forces than the weather;   100
Thy father's thy responsibility.
What happen'd with him earlier today?
Did he, at long last, ask your mother out?

MARTY   [aside:] I've not the heart to tell him truthfully.
Besides, who knows what happen'd once I left?   105
[To Doc:] Methinks he did.

DOC   —Pray tell, what did she say?

                    [Someone knocks on the door of Doc's house.
                              Doc peers through the shade.
It is thy mother, somehow come for thee!
Let's cover up the time machine anon.

                                        [They throw a cover over
                                  the DeLorean. Doc opens the door.
Whatever hell or heaven enters, come.

                    Enter LORRAINE BAINES.

LORRAINE   Hello, sweet Cal—er, Marty.

MARTY   —Ma—Lorraine.   110
How knew'st thou I was here? How hither cam'st?

LORRAINE   I follow'd thy steps homeward, verily.

MARTY   Forgive my manners. This man is my Doc—
My uncle, Doctor Brown.

LORRAINE   —Hello.

DOC   —Good even.

LORRAINE   My manners, Marty, thou too must forgive   115
As I of thee a forward query make:
Wouldst thou ask me to come with thee unto
Th'Enchantment 'Neath the Sea dance Saturday?

MARTY   [aside:] My lie to Doc exposèd in a trice!

[*To Lorraine:*] What, no one hath al̴

LORRAINE   Not yet; I dwell in possibility.
MARTY   Yet what of George?
LORRAINE   —Thou meanest George McFly?
            He hath a somewhat handsome aspect, true,
            But I believe a man should be courageous
            And valiant and strong, e'en as thou art.   125
            A man should take a stand both for himself
            And to protect the woman whom he loves.
            Dost thou not think a true man should be so?
MARTY   When thou dost put it in these simple words,
            Thy meaning's plain. Let us discuss it more.   130
                              [*Exeunt Marty and Lorraine.*
DOC   O, what a tangle hath the young man knit—
            His life dependeth on untying it!
                                              [*Exit.*

SCENE 2

Outside George McFly's house.

Enter MARTY MCFLY *and* GEORGE MCFLY,
hanging laundry on a line together.

GEORGE   Thy words I hear, but little sense they make.
            I prithee, help me understand thee better.
            How can I take Lorraine unto the dance

	When she already eagerly agreed
	To go with thee instead? How shall this work?
MARTY	'Tis plain the lass would rather go with thee,
	Yet may not know the truth of this yet, George.
	This situation we must rectify,
	Unveiling unto her what her heart knows,
	Although her brain is slower to respond.
	We shall show her that thou, strong George McFly,
	Will fight for her, whatever foe may come.
	Thou shalt, then, take a stand both for thyself
	And to protect the woman whom thou lov'st.
	Yea, such a man art thou, of strength and pow'r,
	Courageous in a scuffle 'gainst a brute,
	Jealous in honor, sudden and quick in quarrel.
GEORGE	This generous description makes me smile,
	For gladly would I be the man thou conjur'st,
	Yet never in my life have I rais'd fists
	To start a fight against another person.
MARTY	'Tis not a real fight, Dad—er, Daddy-O.
	Thou comest to her rescue, nothing more.
	Let us review our fail-safe plan again.
	First: at eight fifty-five, where shalt thou be?
GEORGE	I shall be at the merry, hopeless dance.
MARTY	Indeed thou shalt. And where shall I be, then?
GEORGE	Thou shalt be in the car with her: Lorraine.
MARTY	If thou wert scholar, couldst not be more right.
	Around the moment when the clock strikes nine,
	She shall become most furious with me.
GEORGE	This point escapes me—wherefore should she so?
MARTY	George, 'tis a truth attested through the ages
	That gentle lasses angry do become

Line numbers: 5, 10, 15, 20, 25, 30

When men do take advantage of them.
                    [George begins hanging a corset.
GEORGE   —What?   35
These words fall odiously on mine ears.
Thou shalt, then, touch her harshly on her—
                    [Marty takes the corset from
                    George and hangs it up.
MARTY   —Nay!
George, please, believe me when I say these words:
The very thought is sickening to me.
'Tis nothing but an act, is this not so?   40
At nine o'clock, thou strollest through the lot,
And see us struggling there, inside the car.
Thou mak'st a bold approach, and then thou say'st—
                    [Marty pauses, waiting for George.
Now speak, George, 'tis thy cue.
GEORGE   —Of course, indeed!
"Lo, rogue, remove thy filthy, damnèd hands,   45
Release this woman from thy grasp anon!"
Think'st thou 'tis best if I do speak an oath?
MARTY   Yea, George, yea—God damn it, speak thou an oath!
Thou comest thither boldly, to the car,
Then punch me in the stomach and I'll fall.   50
Thine enemy, the brute, is overcome,
And the conclusion is, she shall be thine—
Lorraine and George live happ'ly ever after.
GEORGE   When thou dost tell the tale, it simple sounds,
And yet I wish I were not so afeard.   55
MARTY   Of naught hast thou a reason to be scar'd.
Thou need'st a tittle of self-confidence.
When thou dost put thy mind unto the task,

Thou mayst accomplish nearly anything.
A man of wisdom spoke these words to me,   60
Now may they bring assurance unto thee.

                                        [Exeunt.

SCENE 3

In the town of Hill Valley, near the clock tower.

Enter two POLICEMEN.

POLICE. 1	Good even, Sergeant Bradbury, how art thou?
POLICE. 2	'Tis well, Lieutenant Wells. Thou art well met.
POLICE. 1	How goes the night? Doth anything perturb?
POLICE. 2	Nay, all is well, the evening calm as sleep.
POLICE. 1	Methinks a storm is brewing, is it not?

(5)

POLICE. 2   If so, a butterfly once flapp'd its wings.

POLICE. 1   What meanest thou?

POLICE. 2   —O, understand'st thou not?
See, there's a special providence e'en in
The fall of one small butterfly, forsooth.
A butterfly who flaps its wings, or dies,   10
May have profound effect upon the future—
And e'en upon the weather systems, yea.

POLICE. 1   Is this thy view of traveling through time,
That one may change the future by the past?

POLICE. 2   Indeed. Presume a person travels back,   15
Say thirty years before the present time,

And maketh subtle changes thereupon—
Not e'en a vast change, nay, not murder, theft,
Assassination or a coup d'état—
A simple change, like catching butterflies.   20
Or even something that doth touch the mind:
What if the traveler, whilst in the past,
Did somehow give a person confidence
They never had before? 'Twould change the world—
At least the worlds of those directly touch'd.   25
The person with the greater confidence
Would grow to be e'en more successful than
They'd been before, creating an effect
Like water rippling from a single drop.

POLICE. 1   Is this thy view? 'Tis diff'rent far from mine.   30

POLICE. 2   I'd hear thee more. Canst thou explain to me?

POLICE. 1   We shall employ thine own example, sir.
Suppose a person from a future time,
Who knew the music of their present day,
Did travel back in time and share that music   35
With those who, being thirty years behind,
Had never heard such strains. They would invent
The very music that the traveler
Had come to fancy after thirty years.
The past, in mine example, is not chang'd,   40
But was exactly as it had to be,
Anticipating ev'ry future time,
The cord of fate ne'er alter'd in the least.

POLICE. 2   I see, so thou believ'st the traveler
Hath e'er existed in the past, although   45
They travel'd from the future. Is this so?

POLICE. 1   By mine own view, it is. Yet I would hear

More of thine own opinion on the matter.
Let us talk more and, then, we'll find a snack.

POLICE. 2   Past, present, future—always is it time   50
For coffee and a doughnut. So say I!

[The two policemen step aside to talk more.

Enter MARTY MCFLY *and* DOCTOR EMMETT BROWN,
listening to a weather forecast on the RADIO.

RADIO   The weather in Hill Valley on this night
Is mostly clear, with some few scatter'd clouds.
Our lowest temp'rature tonight shall be
No lower than the forties, Fahrenheit.   55

DOC   Art thou most certain of this storm tonight?
No cloudy show of stormy blust'ring weather
Doth yet in this fair welkin once appear.

MARTY   When was it thou a weatherman didst trust
To read the skies, much less the future tell?   60

DOC   I shall most sorry be to see thee go.
Thou hast giv'n me a target for mine aims,
A vital, noble goal I may pursue.
Now I shall take the road less travel'd by.
That, Marty, hath made all the difference.   65
E'en knowing I, in nineteen eighty-five,
Shall be alive to see profound success,
My greatest labors e'er come to fruition.
One day I shall experience time travel—
Such wondrous expectation, by my troth!   70

MARTY   *[aside:]* Alas, his words do strike my very soul,
As if the man hath died once more just now,
For he shall never know time travel's joy,

	Ne'er eat the hard-won fruit he toil'd to grow.	
DOC	Methinks 'twill be most difficult to wait	75
	Some thirty years before we two can talk	
	O'er all that hath transpir'd these past few days.	
	Most truly shall I miss thee, Marty, aye.	
MARTY	And I shall miss thee, too, more than thou know'st.	
DOC	[*aside:*] Some message hides within young Marty's	
	face,	80
	For all my knowledge, though, I cannot read it.	
MARTY	Doc, hear me speak about what is to be . . .	
DOC	Nay! Que será, será, as we agreed.	
	Should I have information of the future,	
	'Twould be extremely dangerous for me.	85
	E'en if thou hast naught but the best intentions,	
	Remember 'tis with these the road to hell	
	Is often paved. Thine aim, no doubt, is sound,	
	Yet still may backfire most disastrously.	
	Whatever thou dost burn to say to me,	90
	I'll learn within the nat'ral course of time.	

[Marty steps aside.

POLICE. 1	[*approaching:*] Good even, Doctor Brown. What are	
	these wires?	
DOC	A weather trial of mine own devising.	
	[*Aside:*] It could be call'd a whether trial, too,	
	As we discover whether it shall work!	95
POLICE. 1	What is this here, beneath the steely shroud?	
DOC	Nay, do not touch, I prithee. Science 'tis!	
	A tool for weather-sensing specializ'd.	
POLICE. 1	Thou hast, no doubt, a permit for the thing?	
DOC	What dost thou take me for? An amateur?	100
	Come hence, and I shall show thee what thou seek'st.	

It bears the countenance of Andrew Jackson . . .
                    [*Exeunt Doc with policemen.*

MARTY   Doc shall not let my words of future times
             Fall on his ears, if spoken from my lips,
             Yet I must tell him what I, sadly, know.   105
             Another way, perchance, I may employ:
             A letter I shall write for later reading,
             Wherewith Doc's tragic fortune to forfend.
             [*Writing:*] "Dear Doctor Brown—my teacher and my
                                                        friend,
             Upon the night I travel back in time,   110
             Thou shalt be slain by terrorists most vile.
             Please take whate'er precautions necessary
             To keep thyself from this most heinous fate.
             Thy oldest and thy youngest friend, e'en Marty."
             Thus have I writ, to keep kind Doc from harm,   115
             And then inscribe upon the envelope:
             "Ope not until 'tis nineteen eighty-five"—
             E'en thus I hope to keep my friend alive.
                        [*Marty slips the letter in Doc's coat. Exit.*

SCENE 4

In Hill Valley High School at the Enchantment
'Neath the Sea dance, and outside the school.

Enter GEORGE McFLY, *dancing. Enter* MARVIN BERRY
and his merry band THE STARLIGHTERS, *playing music.*

Enter several STUDENTS, *dancing.*

GEORGE   This plan of Marty's brings me little ease;
            I was not fashion'd as a man of action,
            And have but little sense for schemes and ploys.
            Yet if he has it right and through this plot
            I may, incredibly, end up within   5
            The graces of the beautiful Lorraine—
            Preventing thereby, too, Darth Vader's scorn—
            'Twill be worth doing, though I like it not.
            The time is nigh; 'tis now eight fifty-five.
            Lorraine and Marty shall arrive anon,   10
            Then shall our act begin in earnest. O,
            I am afeard of what may come to pass.
            George, screw thy courage to the sticking-place,
            And we'll not fail—good Marty and myself.

Enter MARTY MCFLY *and* LORRAINE BAINES *on balcony, in his car.*

MARTY   We have arriv'd, yet ere we thither go,   15
            Mayhap thou wouldst enjoy it if we park'd.
LORRAINE   Thy mind has mapp'd the perfect path for us,
            For I would gladly park awhile with thee.
MARTY   Indeed? 'Tis not the route I did expect.
LORRAINE   Yea, Marty, I am near eighteen years old;   20
            This isn't the first highway I have travel'd,
            Thy lane is not the first in which I've steer'd.
MARTY   What? Verily? This comes as news to me,
            And reason, probably, to press the brakes.
LORRAINE   Soft, Marty—thou art overheated, dear,   25
            Belike thou shalt thy system flood with nerves.

Is something wrong? Methought we shar'd this hope,
To drive along this road together. Yes?

MARTY   Nay, nay.
                              [Lorraine pulls out a flask and takes a drink.

LORRAINE   —Belike a drink shall brake thy blood.

MARTY   What art thou doing? Drinking whilst thou drive—   30
            Er, whilst we park and rest our engines here.

LORRAINE   I swip'd it from my mother's liquor cupboard.

MARTY   Thou shouldst not drink, else surely thou wilt crash.

LORRAINE   Yet wherefore? Such libation giveth pleasure.

MARTY   Once thou art older, farther down the road,   35
            Thou mayst have some regrets o'er drinking now.

LORRAINE   O Marty, be thy wheels not square, but round,
            Else thou shalt nowhere go. Dost thou not see
            That ev'ryone who's anyone doth drink?
                          [Marty takes a sip as Lorraine pulls out a
                                      cigarette and lights it.

MARTY   What, smoking, too, Lorraine? Dost think it wise?   40
                Shalt not thy young transmission burn withal?

LORRAINE   Thy horn doth bleat much like my mother's sound;
                Betwixt the two of you, my mom and thee,
                I almost cannot tell the difference.

Enter SECOND MARTY MCFLY *on balcony, aside.*

MARTY 2   Bold gentles, patience, as this may confound—   45
                As ye see Marty, stuck inside the car,
                Caught with Lorraine, both mother and admirer,
                Know this: I'm Marty too—or Marty two.
                Ta'en once again to nineteen fifty-five,
                On new adventures hither have I come,   50
                To stop young Biff becoming even worse.
                He hath a book, which I must take away,
                E'en as I do avoid my other self.
                For he is me, yet hath another task—
                Undoing his effect upon Lorraine   55
                To let his father enter in her love.
                Unless I can evade him, all shall fail;
                Relentless is the march of time's harsh rules.
                Excuse my brief intrusion to this scene—
                Think not of me again, I'll not appear.   60
                We shall, perchance, meet in another tale
                Once this is finish'd. Friends, enjoy the show!
                                  [Exit Second Marty.

MARVIN   Young dancers all, 'tis time for us to rest.
                Fear not, for we shall make return anon.
                Fly not, but wait on further melodies.   65

GEORGE   'Tis nine o'clock, and time to be a man.

[Exit George. Exeunt Marvin Berry and the
Starlighters. Lorraine, in the car, takes off her
coat to show her revealing dress.

LORRAINE   Say, Marty, wherefore thou so nervous art?
MARTY   Lorraine, hast thou encounter'd any moment
            Wherein thou must a certain action take,
            Yet when the moment did arrive at last,   70
            Thou wast not sure thou couldst perform the task
            E'en if thou hadst forever and a day?
LORRAINE   Like, mayhap, in what manner one should act,
            Upon a sweet and passionate first date?
MARTY   Yea, very like. O, very like indeed.   75
LORRAINE   Methinks I know exactly what thou mean'st.
MARTY   Dost thou?
LORRAINE   —In situations such as those,
            Canst guess how I comport myself?
MARTY   —Pray tell.
LORRAINE   I worry not o'er what may come to be.
                          [She kisses him. He is stunned.
            Teach not thy lips such scorn, for they were made   80
            For kissing, Marty, not for such contempt.
            Thy visage hath th'appearance of a ghost,
            And ev'rything about this moment flops.
            When I kiss thee, 'tis like I kiss my brother—
            It feels not fancy-free, but filial.   85
            Belike that maketh little sense to thee.
MARTY   Nay, 'tis more sensible than thou dost know.

Enter BIFF TANNEN *on balcony, approaching Marty's car.*
Enter SKINHEAD, 3-D, *and* MATCH *with him. Enter* MARVIN BERRY
and THE STARLIGHTERS *on balcony aside, in another car.*

LORRAINE   With stealthy steps I hear someone approaching.
MARTY   [*aside:*] George comes to end this scene most Oedipal
             Before a tragedy occureth here.   90
                    [*Biff opens the car door and pulls Marty out.*
BIFF   Three hundred ducats' damage to my car
             Thou caus'd, O whoreson small. Now shalt thou pay—
             The sum requir'd is hefty: let the forfeit
             Be nominated for an equal pound
             Of thy fair flesh. I prithee, hold him, lads.   95
MARTY   [*aside:*] How single-minded is his hunt for me,
             An 'twere he had a single eye wherewith
             His tunnel vision only spied revenge.
             No cyclops had more hate for innocence.
                    [*Skinhead, 3-D, and Match hold Marty.*
                                    Biff hits him.
LORRAINE   Release him, Biff! Thou speak'st with drunkard's
                                    tongue. 100
BIFF   Zounds! Look what is herein—a treasure chest.
                            [*Lorraine begins to flee.*
             Nay, thou shalt stay and play with me, Lorraine.
MARTY   Leave her alone, thou base and brutish bastard!
BIFF   Take him around the back—I'll come anon.
             This is no peep show for thy wanton eyes.   105
                    [*Match hits Marty. Skinhead, 3-D, and Match bear
                       him away. Biff and Lorraine struggle in the car.*
SKINHEAD   An open trunk—let's put the knave therein.
3-D   Forsooth!
MATCH   —Ha, ha, a zany plan indeed.
                    [*They throw Marty in the trunk of another car.*
SKINHEAD   'Tis punishment for ruining my hair.

> *[One of the car's doors opens and a member of*
> *the Starlighters emerges.*

STAR. 1   What dost thou to my car, thou wayward youth?

3-D   Be gone, thou spook, for this concerns thee not.   110

> *[The other car doors open. Marvin Berry and*
> *the other Starlighters emerge.*

MARVIN   Who call'st thou spook, thou foolish peckerwood?

SKINHEAD   Take heed unto my voice—I shall not fight
            With dreadful people who live by the pipe!

MARVIN   Fly hence unto thy mama, ignoramus,
            Ere I give thee a knock thou shalt remember.   115

> *[Exeunt Skinhead, 3-D, and Match in fear.*

MARTY   Assist me, please—I'm here, inside the trunk!

MARVIN   Good Reginald, give me thy keys at once.

MARTY   The keys are here, inside the trunk, as well.

MARVIN   Say that again? O, would I heard it wrong.

MARTY   I said the keys are here, inside the trunk.   120

> *[They begin working to set Marty free. Marvin*
> *cuts himself as the trunk opens.*

MARVIN   A-ha, I have it now. O fie, my hand!

MARTY   O, wondrous rescue, friends. Whose keys are these?

STAR. 1   E'en mine.

MARTY   —I must depart. Ye have my thanks.

> *[Exeunt Marvin Berry and the Starlighters.*
> *Exit Marty severally.*

Enter GEORGE MCFLY *on balcony.*

GEORGE   The car. The struggle goeth on inside.
            The time is nine o'clock. The man is I.   125
            The destiny awaiteth, by my troth.

[George opens the door to the car.
    Lo, rogue, remove thy filthy, damnèd hands,
    Release this woman from—alas, 'tis Biff!
BIFF   Methinks thou hast the wrong car found, McFly.
LORRAINE   George, help me, please, if e'er thou likest me.   130
BIFF   Turn thou around, and meekly walk away.
LORRAINE   Please, George.
BIFF   —Art hard of hearing, eh, McFly?
    Close thou the door and thou mayst still escape.
GEORGE   *[aside:]* I shall not let not this bully have his way,
    But summon all the courage I can muster.   135
    [To Biff:] Nay, Biff, it shall not be. Leave her alone.
[Biff emerges from the car.
BIFF   It shall be as you like it, then, McFly.
    Here hast thou ask'd for punishment most grave,
    And thus I shall deliver unto thee.
[George tries to hit Biff,
but Biff grabs his arm and twists it.
LORRAINE   Biff, cease this madness. Thou shalt break his arm!   140
    Leave him alone, thine anger runs too hot.
[Lorraine tries to stop Biff,
who pushes her back into the car.
BIFF   Ha, ha! This is too funny, by my troth!
GEORGE   *[aside:]* O villain, villain, smiling, damnèd villain!
    That one may smile, and smile, and be a villain;
    At least I am sure it may be so in high school.   145
    And here am I, the Arthur to his Mordred,
    The nervous David to his vast Goliath,
    The weaken'd English to the haughty French.
    I'll knock the smile from off his wicked face.
    My fist is like a pistol; shrimps shall rise   150

And make their mark, not be a stepping mat!
Rise, temper that I never felt before,
To give this hateful man what he deserveth.
Yea, here I strike for ev'ry underdog!

Enter MARTY MCFLY *on balcony, hidden.*
GEORGE *hits* BIFF, *who falls to the ground, limp.*

MARTY   [*aside:*] My father, man of strength and valor, too!   155
GEORGE   Lorraine, say, art thou well? Wilt come with me?
LORRAINE   [*aside:*] Ere now I ne'er consider'd George McFly,
Ere now, I never saw him in this light,
Ere now, I never witness'd bravery,
Ere now, I never heard love's tender call.   160
        [*George helps Lorraine out of the car, and they
        exit together.*

Enter two STUDENTS *on balcony.*

STUDENT 1   What happen'd here? Who is that striking man?
STUDENT 2   'Tis George McFly, who here hath vanquish'd Biff.
MARTY   He did it, by my troth, a noble man.
The picture! I must see if it is whole.
        [*Marty looks at the picture.*
Alas, though George hath done the daring deed,   165
The past hath not been fully rectified.
My sister's body halfway disappear'd,
And I am next, unless we make it right.
What can it be that still holds them apart,
Since George hath sav'd Lorraine from Biff's dark
        threat?   170

Of course! My mother often tells the tale
Of how the two of them did first embrace
At the Enchantment 'Neath the Sea. Fly, feet,
Be certain of their love to save my life!
They need to kiss to bolster their romance—   175
The final matter calleth—to the dance!

[*Exeunt.*

SCENE 5

In the town of Hill Valley, near the
clock tower, and Hill Valley High School,
at the Enchantment 'Neath the Sea dance.

Enter DOCTOR EMMETT BROWN *on balcony, near the clock tower.*

DOC   Nine thirty-one, and thunder rumbles gently—
             The storm begins, and lightning follows on.
             The wind doth blow to welcome in the rain,
             Which follows an 'twere night come after day.
             'Tis like young Marty and myself were sailors,   5
             Caught in a storm upon the open sea—
             The Scylla of his parents' fate—and his—
             Would eat his very being happily,
             Whilst the Charybdis of time travel doth
             Attempt to suck us down into the depths.   10
             This tempest will not give me leave to ponder
             On things would hurt me more—on future times,

Of which is Marty keen to tell me much.
'Tis rare a tempest brings a happy end;
Ye gods of cloud and rain, of wind and storm,   15
E'en Zeus, who hurleth lightning to the Earth—
Look favorably now upon our quest.

[Exit Doc.

Enter MARTY McFLY. *Enter* MARVIN BERRY *and*
THE STARLIGHTERS. *Enter* GEORGE McFLY *and* LORRAINE BAINES,
dancing together, and several other STUDENTS, *dancing.*

MARTY   My friends, again we fortunately meet.
               Ye must return inside, and play again—
               The dance must be completed, or all fails.   20
STAR. 1   Look thou on Marvin's hand, with vicious cut.
               He cannot play with such a wound as that,
               And we'll not play without our leading man.
MARTY   O Marvin, thou must play, for when thou dost,
               'Tis then the two shall kiss and fall in love,   25
               Securing mine own future as their son.
               Sans music, there can be no dancing, nay,
               Sans dancing, there shall be no kissing either,
               Sans kissing, there shall be no length of days,
               And the result is this: I'm history.   30
MARVIN   The dance is over, sirrah. Yea, unless
               Thou knowest someone who can play the lute.
MARTY   I can and shall do it—it shall be me—
               I'll pluck the strings e'en for my very life.

[Marty and the Starlighters
begin playing. Marvin sings.

MARVIN   This song we sing for all ye lovers young.   35

[*Singing:*] O mistress mine, Earth angel mine,
    O darling of my heart, I'm thine.
Shalt thou be mine, this year or next,
    Why leave my loving heart perplex'd?
Sing nonny heigh, sing nonny ho,   40
    Earth angel sweet, come dwell below.
O mistress mine, Earth angel mine,
    One I adore, who doth so shine.
'Tis only thee for whom I care,
    And I shall love thee, pet, fore'er.   45
Sing nonny heigh, sing nonny ho,
    Earth angel sweet, come dwell below.

LORRAINE   George, wilt thou kiss me, prithee?

GEORGE   —I know not.
A certain shyness doth befall my spirit.

STUDENT 3   [*approaching:*] Get hence, McFly, I'll claim thy rightful
                                       place. 50
'Tis certain that Lorraine doth want thee not.

                       [*George begins walking away.*]

MARTY   [*aside:*] Why doth he wait? What reason thwarts his
                                    will?
This hesitation causeth strife to me.
Behold my picture: now my sister's gone,
And I begin to disappear as well.   55
Alack, not only on the photograph—
My hand, my right hand—trusted tool of old—
Begins to vanish! Yea, I see straight through't!
The music I play swiftly faltering,
Harmonic chords now turn'd to dissonance.   60
Across the room, I see George turn to go—
Nay, Father, find thy courage, save us all!

STAR. 2   Say, lad, is't well with thee? Hast thou gone sick?

MARTY   I cannot play. I am undone, am finish'd—
              Time's consequences quite o'ercrow my spirit.   65
              I gaze upon the photograph once more,
              Whereon my person whole is nearly gone.
              This is the end for Marty; yea, I die.

LORRAINE   George, leave me not, I bid thee!

MARTY   —Stay, George, stay!
                                      [Marty begins to fall.

GEORGE   [*aside:*] Shall bullies ever have the final say?   70
              They are hard-hearted, mean, and resolute.
              Yet 'tis by fear and sadness they are led—
              Their own uncertainties have made them cruel.
              A bully must be fac'd with courage plain,
              Which doth declare "Thou art not welcome here,"   75
              Ere bullies stop, and healing may begin.
              [*To Student 3:*] Excuse me, sirrah, thou hast ta'en my
                                                              place.
                              *[George pushes Student 3 aside and takes
                                      Lorraine into his arms.*

LORRAINE   I can express no kinder sign of love
              Than this kind kiss.
                                      *[Lorraine and George kiss.
                              Marty is healed immediately and stands.*

GEORGE   —She kisses by the book!

MARTY   O restoration heaven sent, by George!   80
              My body's whole, my spirit made complete.
              My parents—lovely parents, gentle parents,
              Upon the dance floor take their perfect kiss.
              The photograph—what future doth it tell?
              I reappear, with both my siblings too!   85

The rift I made in time hath here been heal'd.
Hands, precious hands, play on these mellow strings,
Support the song that joins these two as one—
If music mark the time of love, play on!
George waves to me, and I—with hand unhurt—   90
Do render back his wave, from friend to friend,
From son to father and from joy to joy.

                                        [*The song ends.*

MARVIN   Well play'd, and thou art passable with th'lute.
           Shall we not play one more? What sayest thou?
MARTY   Nay, nay, for I am almost out of time.   95
MARVIN   Wilt thou be gone? It is not yet near day:

It was the nightingale, and not the lark,
That pierced the fearful hollow of thine ear;
Nightly she sings on yon pomegranate-tree:
Believe me, sirrah, 'twas the nightingale. 100
Let us play aught to match the bird's sweet song—
A melody with vim and vigor fill'd!

MARTY   [*aside:*] An audience who'd gladly hear me play?
Is this not what I long'd for in my time?
[*To Marvin:*] A melody with vim and vigor, eh? 105
The perfect song doth spring into my mind.

MARVIN   'Tis well—take thou the microphone, and speak.

MARTY   [*to all:*] Forsooth, this is an oldie whence I come.
Men, follow on—a riff of blues in B,
Which changeth quickly. Watch me carefully, 110
For I shall be thy guide and leader both.
See if thy rhythms can keep pace with mine!
              [*Marty begins playing. All dance.*

MARVIN   The music is unknown, yet doth delight.
Play on, my boys, we shall take joy tonight!

MARTY   [*singing:*] Upon a hidden lane, in deepest wood, 115
Was born a child who play'd as no one could.
His genius was pronounc'd e'en from boyhood—
His name was Jonathan Bernardo Goode.
    How good when Goode begins to play the lute,
    Sing ho, sing high, sing heigh! 120
They took him from his humble neighborhood,
To play withal the king's court, if he would.
By queens his gift was lauded as it should—
No one was better, nay—'twas understood.
    How good when Goode begins to play the lute, 125
    Sing ho, sing high, sing heigh!

STUDENT 4   Bold George, I heard thou didst give Biff a knock—
             Well done, brave soul, for 'twas long overdue.
STUDENT 5   Hast thou e'er thought of running for the post
             Of president of all the senior class?   130
             We need someone of thine integrity!
GEORGE   [*aside:*] O, how my prospects chang'd in one fell
                                                             swoop!
                         [*Marvin walks to a nearby telephone.*
MARVIN   Although this music ringeth in mine ears
             Profoundly, as none other did before,
             It may, perchance, become a new sensation.   135
             I'll ring, upon the telephone, anon,
             My cousin Chuck, a songwriter most clever.
             Methinks he shall enjoy this newfound sound,
             Releasing it unto the masses. [*Into phone:*] Chuck?
             'Tis Marvin. Marvin who? 'Tis Marvin Berry,   140
             Thy cousin since thou wert a little boy.
             Think back upon what thou and I discuss'd—
             Inventing some new sound to change the world—
             I'll wager thou shalt thrill at what I've found!
             Now hear this music and be thou amaz'd.   145
                         [*Marvin holds out the phone. Marty begins
                                    playing wildly. All stare.*
MARTY   The future comes too swiftly hereupon.
             Apologies, companions, for this slip,
             For by thy disapproving visages
             I see thou art not ready for these sounds;
             Methinks the generation next shall be.   150
                         [*The dance resumes as the Starlighters play
                         again. Marty begins walking out and is stopped
                                         by Lorraine and George.*

LORRAINE	The music was most interesting, Marty,
	Not good, nay. No. But interesting 'twas.
MARTY	Judicious are thy words, just shy of praise.
LORRAINE	Beg pardon, Marty, yet, if thou mind'st not,
	George ask'd if he could take me home tonight. 155
MARTY	Such news rings like the sweetest bells of heav'n
	That e'er did ring upon a bleak man's ears!
	'Tis well; about you two I feel encourag'd.
LORRAINE	Yea, as do I, though I do blush to say't.
MARTY	I must depart anon, yet hear my words: 160
	To meet thee hath been educational.
LORRAINE	Shall we e'er see thee more within this life?
MARTY	Indeed, I guarantee thou shalt, Lorraine—
	The picture of the future I can see.
GEORGE	O Marty, many thanks for thine advice— 165
	Ne'er shall it be forgotten all my days.
MARTY	A pleasure 'twas, brave George. Good luck to ye.

[Marty turns to leave, then stops.

	A final word, I pray, ere I fly hence:
	If ever you have children—nay, blush not,
	Though now 'tis but a glimmer in your eyes— 170
	If one of them, when he is eight years old,
	Doth set afire the carpet in your room,
	Will ye with mercy look upon the boy?
GEORGE	Whate'er these words do presage, we agree!

[Exit Marty.

LORRAINE	A pleasant name is Marty, by my troth, 175
	A name to foster loyalty and growth.

[Exeunt, holding hands.

SCENE 6

In the town of Hill Valley, near the clock tower.
The storm brews.

Enter DOCTOR EMMETT BROWN.

DOC   The time, it is upon us—where's the boy?
         Nine fifty-six, and tell me—where's the boy?
         We've fewer than ten minutes—where's the boy?
         The storm begins to brew—damn! Where's the boy?

Enter MARTY McFLY.

         Th'art late, e'en for a most important date!   5
         Hast thou but little concept of time's rush?
MARTY   Forgive me, for I had to change my garb.
         Think'st thou I shall go back in such a suit?
         Mine old man did the deed—the plan hath work'd!
DOC   Do tell!
MARTY   —In just one punch he laid out Biff,   10
         Game, set, and match, all in a single blow.
         I never knew he had the inner strength.
         Ne'er hath the man stood up to brutish Biff.
                      [Marty hands Doc the photograph.
DOC   The photo is intact. Thus, all is well.
         Yet "ne'er," thou sayest, ne'er hath he done so?   15
MARTY   Nay, wherefore askest thou? What is the matter?
DOC   *[aside:]* What may a man with greater courage do
         Than he hath done before? Ah, time will tell.

[*To Marty:*] Pay it no mind. Let's get thee back anon:
First, let us set thy destination time.   20
                              [*They open the door of the DeLorean.*
This readout showeth just when thou didst leave.
We'll send thee back upon the very instant—
'Twill be as though thou never didst depart.
Thou must drive yonder, past the bold white line,
Which I already painted on the street.   25
It doth demark the starting line for thee.
The distance most precise I've calculated,
Giv'n wind's sharp turns, acceleration speed,
All retroactive to the moment when
The lightning bolt shall strike the tower here—   30
In minutes seven, seconds twenty-two.
When this alarm doth ring, depress the gas!

MARTY   'Tis well thought out as all thy schemes are, Doc.
DOC   My words are finish'd; all is set in place.
MARTY   My thanks, sweet Doc.
DOC   —Thanks unto thee, my friend. 35
                              [*Marty embraces Doc.*
         I'll see thee once again—in thirty years.
MARTY   Thus do I hope, most fervently.
DOC   —Fear not.
         An thou but hit the wire with this long hook,
         Whilst driving eighty-eight in miles per hour,
         The instant that the lightning strikes the tower—   40
         All shall be well, all shall be well, yea, and
         All manner of things shall be well, forsooth.
                     [*Marty sits in the DeLorean. Doc notices the
                                        letter in his pocket.*
         Wait, what is this? What words are written here?

"Ope not until 'tis nineteen eighty-five"?
What meaneth this?

MARTY   —Find out in thirty years.   45

DOC   These works speak of the future, do they not?
'Tis information of our days to come.
O Marty, heard'st thou naught of what I said?
What if the Trojans knew the Greeks' deception?
How might the destiny of Troy been chang'd?   50
What if the Hun had known the future, eh?
What greater conquests might he have achiev'd?
What if bold Caesar knew what was to be?
Belike his empire still might reign today!
Did I not warn thee of the danger, lad?   55
The consequences could be most disastrous!

MARTY   The risk is one that must be taken, Doc.
Thy very life dependeth on the risk.

                    [Doc begins to rip open the letter.

DOC   Nay! I'll bear not th'responsibility.

MARTY   In that case, I shall tell thee here and now!   60

                    [Lightning strikes a nearby tree. It falls on Doc's
                              cord, knocking it down.

DOC   Great Scott! The cord we need hath come unplugg'd.
No more of future speech: take thou the cable,
And I shall throw the rope to thee.

MARTY   —Indeed!

                    [Doc ascends the clock tower, climbing to the
                              balcony. The storm grows louder.

DOC   How high this tower is above the street!
How many gears do work their steady tasks.   65
I am afeard, yet have no time for doubt.
Upon the precipice I deftly walk—

The lightning bursts—a gargoyle's face! Alack!
Was ever science frightening as this?

MARTY   Canst hear me, Doc? I prithee, throw the rope.   70

> *[Doc tosses a long rope to Marty, who ties the*
> *cord to it.*

DOC   Be swift, young Marty.

MARTY   —Done! Now, pull it hence!

> *[Doc pulls the rope, with the cord tied to it,*
> *toward him.*

E'en if it must be shouted, hear these words:
I must tell thee about the future!

DOC   —What?

MARTY   About the future I must tell thee, Doc!

DOC   Thou art too far away, I cannot hear!   75

MARTY   Thou shalt, upon the night when I return—

> *[The clock begins tolling.*

DOC   O, hear the loud alarum of the bells—
What tale of fright their turbulency tells!

MARTY   Doc is affrighted so, I fear he'll fall.

DOC   The clock strikes ten o'clock—thou must depart!   80
No more of yelling words I cannot hear,
But four mere minutes stands betwixt thee and
The possibility of thy success!
Behold the time and fly ere 'tis too late!

> *[Marty gets into the DeLorean and drives to the*
> *starting point.*

I'll see thee in a trice and then no more   85
Until some thirty years have wander'd by.
Godspeed! Yet, while I wait, I have a task:
I must connect these cords an this shall work.
Near doth one dangle, opposite the face,

As if it taunted me, just out of reach.   90
My face and body must traverse the clock
To get the cord connected once again.
Alack, my foot doth slip, I nearly fall!
Pray, get a grip most literally, Doc.
Walk carefully—each step means life or death.   95
The clock's face and mine own now face each other,
Two faces join'd together for a kiss—
The kiss of cord to cord and plan to feat.

MARTY   Here stand I at the starting line, prepar'd!
The hook I'll raise to catch the lightning's pow'r.   100
Yet how shall I save Doc? What shall I do?
The storm kept him from hearing my report.
Damn, Doc, why didst thou tear the letter up?
Why tear thy hopes of living into pieces?
Why tear thy future from a better path?   105
Why tear my heart, which shall lose thee once more?
If I had but more time—more time, 'tis all.
Yet wait—what words do issue from my mouth?
I have a time machine! I've all the time
That e'er hath been, if I but make it mine.   110
'Tis simple—I shall earlier return,
That I may locate Doc and give him warning.
Ten minutes should be all I need, forsooth—
Whole nations fell in less a time than that.
I shall reset the input, ha! 'Tis done.   115
The circuits for the time all function well,
The flux capacitor, it fluxeth on,
The engine running, let the plan proceed!
                              [The engine of the car dies.
Nay, nay, how canst thou fail at such a time?

DOC   Alas, I fall again, the ledge doth break,   120
           For 'twas not made for bearing human weight!
           First face to face, O clock, now hand to hand:
           I take its hands to save myself from death.
                            [The alarm clock in the DeLorean rings.

MARTY   Fie on it! Start, thou damnèd gray machine.
           This ringing is Doc's signal for my start.   125
           If thou work not, I'll strike thee, by my troth!
                            [Marty hits his head against the steering wheel,
                                              and the car starts.

           By Jove, it worketh! Ha! Feet, press the gas,
           And start the journey homeward presently!

DOC   One cord hath caught my cuff, which starts to rip,
           I grab one cord and, hanging from it, grasp—   130
           Now are both cords within my reach at last.
           O, link them swiftly, Doc, and all is well.
           What newfound thorn is this, deep in my flesh?
           They do not reach! By some six inches short!
           Pull, pull! Give me the slack I need, I beg!   135
           A-ha! 'Tis done! The span now long enow.
           Yet O, the act is not sans consequence—
           Forsooth, another pair is torn asunder!
           Below me, by the sidewalk, hath the cord
           Which first was trapp'd beneath a falling tree,   140
           Unfasten'd from its mate! I must hie down,
           To fix a split connection once again.
           The clock strikes ten oh two—no more delay:
           There is the car, approaching me with haste!
           Be firm and resolute, or all is lost.   145

MARTY   The speed to sixty-one, now sixty-two.
           Accelerate unto thy destiny!

Into the seventies the car doth fly,
My heart is racing in mine anxious chest,
As if it plann'd to pace the speeding car!   150

DOC   Quick! Fashion I a line to slide upon,
And I'll slip down to fix the broken spot.
This could be fun, if 'twere not critical.

    [Doc hangs a wire on one clock hand and slides
         down the wire to the ground.

MARTY   There's Doc, and doth he still the cords repair?
Fail not, brave scientist and treasur'd friend.   155
My eighty-eight in miles per hour achiev'd,
'Tis set! If it be now, 'tis not to come;
If it be not to come, it will be now;
If it be not now, yet it still will come:
The readiness is all.

DOC   —'Tis ten oh four!   160
The lightning strikes, I join the parted cords.

    [There is a burst of lightning. Exit Marty in the
         DeLorean, as it travels back through time.

A crash of drums, a flash of light, my time
Machine flies out of sight! It work'd; it works!
All that remaineth are two fiery streaks,
And of our triumph all creation speaks!   165

                     [Exit.

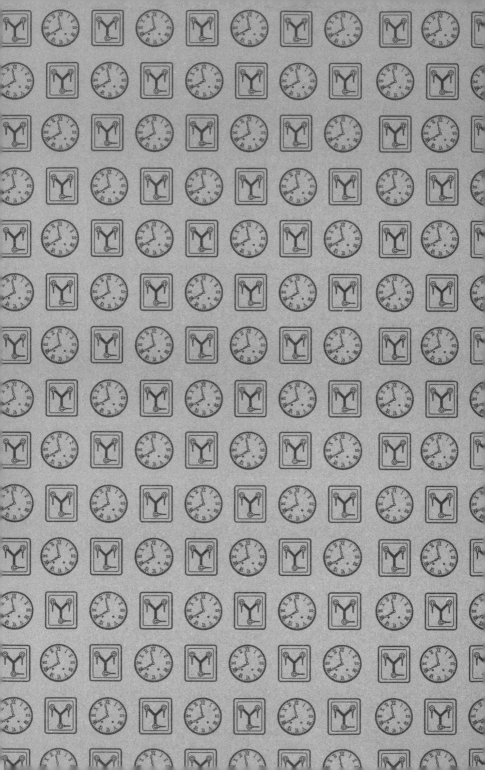

ACT V

SCENE 1

The year 1985. Hill Valley, near the clock tower.

Enter MARTY MCFLY *in the DeLorean,*
with a DRUNK MAN *aside, sleeping. He wakes.*

MAN   And what's he then who says I play the drunkard?
               For here's one sodden wholly by his cup,
               Who then behind a wheel did choose to ride.
               To drive whilst drinking—'tis a madness vile.
                        [Exit man. Marty opens the DeLorean's door.
MARTY   I see around me all the marks of home.   5
               Redhair, the drunkard, passing by my path,
               Our theater which showeth naughty shows,
               The whole town fill'd with litter, as I know't—
               Hill Valley, by my troth, my perfect home.
               One twenty-four—I still have time for Doc.   10
               Straight to the mall, where I shall rescue him.
                        [Marty tries to start the car, but it will not start.
               The engine starteth not—O, rue the day!

Enter two LIBYANS, *passing by in their van.*

LIBYAN 1   To victory, my brother—and revenge!
                        [Exeunt Libyans.
MARTY   The Libyans—alas, I am too late.
               I shall unto the mall make way by foot,   15
               And peradventure still may beat them there.
                        [Marty runs to the mall.

The sign says Lone Pine Mall, not Twin Pines, strange—
Have all my memories chang'd?

Enter DOCTOR EMMETT BROWN, SECOND MARTY MCFLY,
EINSTEIN, *and two* LIBYANS.

LIBYAN 1	*[to Doc:]*	—Justice 'tis.
		[Libyan 1 shoots Doc.
MARTY 2	Nay! Bastard base!	
LIBYAN 1	—Why bastard? Wherefore base?	
	[The scene plays out as before, in pantomime,	
	with Marty watching.	

MARTY   Doc slain again, before my tardy eyes!   20
Nay! Say it is not so, O Fates unfair.
The scene entire is acted out once more,
Yet now am I become a spectator.
How close I came to death I now may see,
Though in the moment's rush I knew it not.   25
How chance did intervene to keep me safe,
Lest I should share a tragic end with Doc.

The time machine, I see it racing off—
I wanted only to escape, and had
No notion of th'adventure I would have.   30

              . [The DeLorean disappears in a flash.
           The Libyans, surprised, crash their van into
                  a photo-processing booth.

The chase is o'er, the car hath disappear'd,
Gone hence in time to nineteen fifty-five.
The Libyans crash in a blazing pyre,
Methinks I am not sad to see them thus.
To Doc now, quickly, so that I may see   35
If there be signs of life within him yet.

                      [Marty runs to Doc.

Doc! Doc! O, fie! I was not fast enow.
For thee I ne'er did have the chance to grieve.

                [Doc rises, slowly, stunned.

By heav'n, thou art alive! How can this be?

         [Doc opens his shirt to reveal a bulletproof vest.

A tunic fashion'd to repel a bullet!   40
How didst thou know what danger thou wouldst face?
I never had the chance to counsel thee.

              [Doc pulls a letter from his coat.

DOC   A letter I received, from friend most true,
And sav'd some thirty years to show it thee.
This night, thy words have sav'd my grateful life.   45

MARTY   What of the danger thou hast caution'd me—
The past and future in a dodgy mix,
With grave effect and horrid consequences
On the continuum of time and space—
Of which I did so often hear thee tell?   50

DOC   Methought upon it and said, "What the hell?"

Come now, and I shall take thee safely home,
And finally my future journey take.

MARTY   How far ahead imaginest thou'lt go?

DOC   A span of thirty years doth have a ring—   55
It work'd for thee and may yet work for me.

MARTY   When thou arrivest, look for me, I pray.
I shall be forty-seven by that time.

DOC   Of course I shall, my true and constant friend.

MARTY   Take care.

DOC   —Thou also, Marty. Now, farewell.   60

MARTY   O furry Einstein, keep good watch.

EINSTEIN   —Woof, woof!⁵

MARTY   One last thing, Doc, beware of thy reentry.
It giveth one a bump to shake one's soul.

DOC   I shall. Off to the future fly we two!

                [Exit Marty.

O Einstein, what adventures we shall have   65
As we confront two thousand and fifteen.
What shall the world be like in thirty years?
More peaceful, I've no doubt, than it is now,
Our country likely unified as one,
With squabbles and disputes political   70
As rare as poverty, which shall, I'll wager,
Be seen upon the planet nevermore.
Utopia 'twill be, if I've a guess—
Of humankind I do expect no less!

                [Exeunt.

---

⁵ *Editor's translation*: So shall I, Marty, and keep our Doc safe.
My bold and playful canine spirit trust,
For I am man's best friend—this funny man,
This brave and noble man, this clever man.

SCENE 2

At the McFly house.

Enter MARTY MCFLY, *awaking.*

MARTY   The sleep of seven bodies I have had—
               So soundly rested like I never knew
               The pleasure of a full night's sleep till now.
               The clock doth tell me 'tis ten twenty-eight—
               I've slept so late, I near have miss'd the day.   5
               What strange remembrance leaps into my mind:
               A sudden jaunt to nineteen fifty-five,
               My parents young, my very life at risk,
               My good friend Doc first kill'd and then alive—
               My troublous dream this night doth make me sad.   10
                              [He walks out of his room
                              and sits on a stool in the kitchen.
               What is this furniture I see herein?
               We do not own such fancy, costly things!

Enter DAVE *and* LINDA MCFLY, *both dressed nicely.*

LINDA   I prithee, Dave, when Paul doth call on me,
               Wilt tell him I work late at the boutique?
DAVE   Sweet sister, I am not thy secretary,   15
               And what of Greg or Craig who just hath call'd?
LINDA   Thou must be more specific: Greg or Craig?
DAVE   I do not know—thy boyfriends countless are.
MARTY   Holla! What is this scene ye two do play?

LINDA	'Tis breakfast—nothing more and nothing less.	20
DAVE	Hast thou once more been sleeping in thy clothes?	
MARTY	Indeed. What are these garments thou dost wear?	
DAVE	It is my custom thus to be array'd	
	When I unto my bus'ness office go.	
	Art thou all right?	
MARTY	—Methinks so. Or shall be.	25

Enter GEORGE *and* LORRAINE MCFLY, *holding tennis equipment.*

LORRAINE	I'll wager thou must grant to me a rematch!	
GEORGE	A rematch—wherefore, dear? Say, didst thou cheat?	
LORRAINE	Nay, sweet one.	
GEORGE	—Well, hello.	
LORRAINE	—Good morning, all.	
	[Marty falls to the floor in surprise.	
MARTY	Sweet Mother! Father!	
GEORGE	—Didst thou hit thy head?	
LORRAINE	O, art thou well, my gentle youngest child?	30
MARTY	You two look wonderful, and Mom—so thin!	
LORRAINE	My thanks, good Marty. [*George pinches her.*] O, you	
	rascal, George!	
	Good morning, sleepyhead. Ho, Dave and Linda.	
DAVE	Good morning, Mother.	
LINDA	—Greetings to you both.	
	I nearly had forgotten, brother Marty:	35
	Your girlfriend Jennifer hath call'd on thee.	
LORRAINE	She is so dear a lass; I like her so.	
	Is not tonight the night of thy big date?	
MARTY	What hast thou spoken, Mother? Say again?	
LORRAINE	Are ye not headed for the lake tonight?	40

	Thou hast been planning for a fortnight's span.
MARTY	Did we not speak about this, Mother dear?
	How shall we to the lake? The car is wreck'd.
GEORGE	'Tis wreck'd?
DAVE	—What is this wreck'd?
LINDA	—What happen'd to't?
DAVE	When hath this awful accident occurr'd? 45
GEORGE	Be silent, all. The car is surely fine.
DAVE	Why am I ever last to know such things?

Enter BIFF TANNEN, *outside,*
waxing the McFlys' car.

GEORGE	Behold, big Biff, who waxeth presently.
	[*To Biff:*] Take careful heed unto my words now, Biff,
	We shall have two full coats of wax this time, 50
	Not only one as thou hast done before.
BIFF	The second layer I am just completing.
GEORGE	Biff, nay—I'll none of thy dissembling words.
BIFF	Good sir McFly, apologies I render—
	I should have said the second was just started. 55
GEORGE	That Biff, a funny character indeed—
	E'er trying to mislead and get ahead.
	Since high school I have had to watch his moves.
	Yet, if he ne'er had enter'd our two lives—
LORRAINE	Ne'er would we two have fallen deep in love. 60
GEORGE	Thou hast it right, my one and only love.
	[*Biff enters the house carrying a box.*
BIFF	My patient sir, this minute hath a package
	Arriv'd for thee—a box most full and heavy.
	Good morning, Marty! 'Tis, methinks, thy newest—

The clever book thou hast been long expecting.   65
          [George and Lorraine open
                  the package together.

LORRAINE   My dearest, thy first novel come at last!
             A *Match Compos'd in Space,* by George McFly.

GEORGE   'Tis like the simple words I ever say:
             When thou dost put thy mind unto the task,
             Thou mayst accomplish nearly anything.   70
                 [Biff hands Marty a set of keys.

BIFF   Good Marty, take the keys thou shalt be needing—
             Thou art all wax'd and ready for this evening.
                 [Exeunt Dave, Linda, and Biff.
                 George and Lorraine stand aside while
                 Marty walks to the garage. He opens
                 the door to reveal a black truck.

MARTY   Is all my dreaming suddenly come true?

Enter JENNIFER PARKER.

JENNIFER	Shall thou give me a ride, thou handsome man?
MARTY	Sweet Jennifer, of women thou art first: 75
	Intelligence to put the wise to shame,
	Good humor rife with educated wit,
	Compassion as would move a saint to tears,
	And beauty that would make e'en Helen green.
	How, like a balm upon my weary soul, 80
	The sight of thee doth fall upon mine eyes.
	Within thy smile, I see our future plain:
	Our wooing whilst our fervent youth remains,
	Our courtship when we both are budding scholars,
	Our romance growing with the passing months. 85
	My Jennifer, when trouble comes along,
	Disrupting the skill'd pilot of our love—
	Thou shalt, as if thou wert a captain brave,
	Steer us to calmer seas and safer shores,
	Wherein our love may dock with confidence. 90
	Thou shalt create a bargain with Poseidon,
	Employing all thy tools of navigation:
	Forgiveness as the compass of the heart,
	Unending grace to act as rudder sure,
	And love that serves as ship and mast and hull— 95
	The vessel that doth keep us always safe.
	Kind Jennifer, we shall support each other
	Through all the trials of the turning world.
JENNIFER	Sweet Marty, such a speech and such a welcome.
	Thou look'st on me as though I'd hid from thee, 100
	And in full seven days hast seen me not.
MARTY	So have I not. At least, 'tis so to me.

JENNIFER   Love, art thou well? Does all proceed aright?
                      [George and Lorraine wave at Marty and
                                                        exeunt.

MARTY   My parents whole, my life somehow improv'd—
             Yea, ev'rything is wondrous in th'extreme.   105
                                                [They kiss.

Enter DOCTOR EMMETT BROWN, *strangely clad, arriving from the*
future in the DeLorean.

DOC   O Marty, thou must voyage hence with me!
MARTY   Where shall we go?
DOC   —Once more back to the future.
                      [Doc rummages through a trash can.
MARTY   What art thou doing, Doc? What is thy plan?
DOC   Some useless refuse must I use anon:
             Thereby I shall fill Mister Fusion up,   110
             That I may have the necessary fuel.
             Home energy reactors useful are!
             I prithee, quickly climb inside the car.
MARTY   Nay, Doc. I have but lately here arriv'd.
             My Jennifer is here, and we are bound   115
             To take my newfound truck and yonder drive.
DOC   Bring her withal, for this concerns her too.
MARTY   Of what art thou most vaguely speaking, Doc?
             What shall befall us in the coming years?
             If we are changed to aught, is't to an ass?   120
DOC   Nay, Marty, ye do flourish, by my troth.
             It is your children who are my concern.
             We must do something for your children. See?
MARTY   Though we may understand it not, we'll go.

[Marty and Jennifer climb into the car.
Doc, we've no room upon this shorten'd street.   125
Go farther back, I pray, an thou wouldst have
Enow of road to realize eighty-eight.

DOC   Be ready for audacious episodes—
Whither we go, we have no need of roads.

[The DeLorean rises into the air and flies away.
Exeunt omnes.

END.

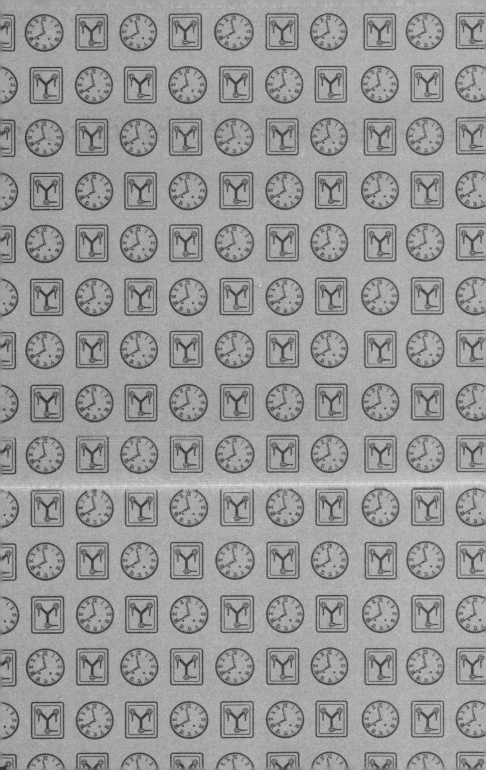

AFTERWORD

Back to the Future has been one of my favorite films since its 1985 debut. I was eight years old at the time, and I loved the movie from the first time I watched it. The DeLorean was *awesome*, Michael J. Fox and Christopher Lloyd were hilarious, and the story was incredibly entertaining. We bought the movie on VHS, of course, and I watched it regularly.

For years, people have been asking me, "Will you ever write a Shakespearean adaptation other than *Star Wars*?" The truth is that, for a long time, I didn't know. Several movies and television series have been recommended to me, and *Back to the Future* was a frequent suggestion. When Quirk Books called and asked me if I was interested in bringing my Shakespearean quill (it's really a laptop) to *Back to the Future*, I didn't take long to answer.

Observant readers, especially those who know their Shakespeare, will notice a few special touches throughout this book. Marty has two speeches that are quite lengthy; in fact, they are each exactly eighty-eight lines long, for obvious reasons. In Act I, when we first meet George and Biff, George's lines of iambic pentameter all have an additional, eleventh syllable, which scholars refer to as a "weak" ending because the line ends on a nonstressed syllable. Biff's lines contrast with George's in that scene, all ending on stressed syllables (the norm for iambic pentameter). In Act V, when their roles are reversed, their rhythms are, too: Biff's lines have weak endings and George enjoys strong ones.

Something you may not have noticed is that the first letters of certain speeches form an acrostic. The first instance is in the chorus prologue, at the beginning of the story; read the first letter of each line to see what it spells out. Then hunt for two other acrostics hidden in the book.

Back to the Future's soundtrack includes many classic songs, and I tried to pay homage to all of them as best I could. This includes giving Huey Lewis's famous cameo a series of lines inspired by Lewis's song catalog (in the film, he's the one who tells Marty his music is "too darn loud"). Finally, in Act IV I gave dialogue not found in the movie to two minor characters; this continues a tradition I started in my William Shakespeare's Star Wars books.

While working on this project, I noticed how completely Marty McFly stands at the center of the movie. Most scenes begin and end with him in the shot. This raised a few challenges in rewriting the story as a play. In a theatrical production, the last person on stage in one scene rarely is the first person to enter in the next scene; the actors need a chance to change costumes or set up for the next scene. I tried my hardest to make sure that an actor portraying Marty on stage would have breathing room between such appearances, which often meant ending or starting a scene with another character's soliloquy.

Thanks for joining me on this journey through time. Where will the future take us? What's coming next in the space-time continuum? Your guess is as good as mine. But I'm certain that wherever we're going, even if we don't need roads we'll still need Shakespeare.

ACKNOWLEDGMENTS

Thank you:

To my parents Bob and Beth Doescher, my brother Erik, his wife Em, and my nieces Aracelli and Addison.

To the team at Quirk Books: Rick Chillot, Nicole De Jackmo, Brett Cohen, Jhanteigh Kupihea, Christina Schillaci, Kelsey Hoffman, Ivy Weir, Jane Morley, Doogie Horner, and the rest of the crew.

To Josh Hicks. I'm sorry I punched you in the arm in 1994.

To the Brooklyn Park Pub writing group, who let me crash their party: Tom George, Kristin Gordon, Chloe Ackerman, and Graham Steinke.

To wonderful friends who provide support and laughter: Heidi Altman and Scott Roehm, Jane Bidwell, Murray Biggs, Travis Boeh and Sarah Woodburn, Chris Buehler and Marian Hammond, Erin and Nathan Buehler, Melody and Jason Burton, Emily and Josiah Carmi- nati, Jeff and Caryl Creswell, Joel Creswell and Sibyl Siegfried and Sophie, Katherine Creswell and Spencer Nietmann, Jeanette Ehmke, Mark Fordice, Holly Havens, Mona and Roland Havens, Jim and Nancy Hicks, Anne Huebsch, Apricot, David, Isaiah and Oak Irving, Jerryn Johnston, Alexis Kaushansky and Ruby, Chris and Andrea Martin, Bruce McDonald, Joan and Grady Miller, Tara and Michael Morrill, Lucy and Tim Neary, Dave Nieuwstraten, Omid Nooshin, Bill Rauch, Julia Rodriguez-O'Donnell, Helga, Michael, and Isabella Scott, David and Sarah Shepherd, J.C. Smith, J. Thomas, Naomi Wal- cott and Audu Besmer, Ryan, Nicole, Mackinzie, Audrey and Lily Warne-McGraw, Steve Weeks, Ben and Katie Wire, Ethan Younger- man and Rebecca Lessem, and Dan Zehr.

To my spouse Jennifer, who told me she "might actually read this one." She is the best partner a guy could want and loves me even when one (or both) of us is tired, hungry, or cranky. To my sons Liam and Graham, who are both teenagers now and helpfully remind me how old I am and how thin my hair is getting. Thank you, boys. Your old bald dad loves you.

READER'S GUIDE

You don't need to be a Shakespeare scholar to enjoy *William Shakespeare's Get Thee Back to the Future*. But if you've come to this book with more knowledge about Marty McFly than the Bard of Avon, this reader's guide may help deepen your understanding of the language and structure of the book, all of which is inspired by Shakespeare's work.

Iambic Pentameter

Shakespeare wrote his plays in a specific syllabic pattern known as iambic pentameter. An *iamb* is a unit of meter, sometimes called a foot, consisting of two syllables, the first of which is unstressed, or soft, and the second of which is stressed, or emphasized. Together the two syllables of an iamb sound like "da-DUM," as in beyond ("be-YOND"), across ("a-CROSS"), and McFly ("mick-FLY"). *Pentameter* is a line of verse containing five feet. So iambic pentameter consists of five iambs, or ten syllables alternating in emphasis. A famous example of this meter, with the stressed half of each iamb in bold, is:

I'd **rath**er **be** a **ham**mer **than** a **nail**.

However, as much as we associate Shakespeare with iambic pentameter, he broke the rule almost as much as he observed it. The most famous Shakespearean line of all has eleven syllables, not ten: "To **be** or **not** to **be**, that **is** the **ques**tion." That last *-ion* is known as a weak ending, or an unstressed syllable. Shakespeare often used weak endings, added two unstressed syllables where there should be one, and left out syllables.

Let's see iambic pentameter in action with this speech from Act III, scene 2 (see page 87).

MARTY	Nay, Doc, I yet may prove I speak the truth.	
	The bruise thou hast, upon thy head of white,	
	I know whence it hath come, yea, and wherefore;	
	Thou didst unfold to me the tale entire.	
	Upon the precipice of thy commode.	80
	Thou stood'st, intent to fix a timepiece there.	
	Thou fell'st and knock'dst thy head upon the sink.	
	Then did a picture come into thy mind:	
	Thy miracle, the flux capacitor,	
	Which maketh possible time travel. Truly,	85
	Believ'd I not before, yet now I do.	

If you read this speech aloud, you may notice that the dialogue sounds unnatural if spoken according to how the individual lines are broken. Rather, punctuation should guide how lines of iambic pentameter are spoken, as if the speech were written as prose. Consider lines 84–86: "Thy miracle: the flux capacitor, / Which maketh possible time travel. Truly, / Believ'd I not before, yet now I do." These two sentences are split across three lines and, when read, each line should naturally flow into the next. (By the way, line 85 contains an example of a weak ending.)

What about words with more than two syllables? The trick with multisyllabic words is to figure out which syllable in the word has the primary emphasis. Let's consider the word *plutonium*: The primary emphasis is normally on the second syllable, plutonium. In iambic pentameter, it makes sense to pronounce it as two iambs, "pluto-" and "-nium." The final syllable -*um* provides a secondary stress that fits the meter nicely.

To Thee or Not to Thee?

Shakespeare's work is well known to be full of archaic pronouns (think *thee* and *thou*) and verbs ending in *-est* and *-eth* that can sound jarring to a modern ear. Consider this your crash course in these unfamiliar terms.

- **thou:** second person singular pronoun that's the subject of a sentence, as in "Thou art predictable as time itself." Modern writers would use *you*.
- **thee:** second person singular pronoun that's the object of a sentence, as in "Get thee back to the future." Modern writers would use *you*.
- **ye:** second person plural pronoun that's either the subject or object of a sentence. Modern writers would use *you*.
- **thy:** second person singular possessive before a word starting with a consonant, as in "thy head." Modern writers would use *your*.
- **thine:** second person singular possessive before a word starting with a vowel, as in "thine assistance." Modern writers would use *your*.

In general, the *-est* ending (sometimes shortened, with an apostrophe, to *-st* or just *-t*) is added to a verb whose subject is the pronoun *thou*: "Thou didst" or "thou stood'st." The *-eth* ending accompanies verbs whose subject is *he* or *she* or a singular *it*: "It groweth closer, like a comet that / Doth make its way across the starry heav'ns."

Another note about verb endings: In Shakespeare's time, the *-ed* at the end of a past tense verb was sometimes pronounced as a separate syllable. Whereas a modern speaker would pronounce the word *believed* as two syllables, back then people would have pronounced three syllables: "be-liev-ed." When such a word needed to be shortened to fit the meter, Shakespeare wrote it as a contraction: *believ'd*. In modern editions of Shakespeare—and in *William Shakespeare's Get Thee Back to the Future*—an accent over the *e* indicates that the *-ed* should be pronounced as a separate syllable: *believèd*.

Other Shakespearean Hallmarks

The following features of a Shakespearean play are all found in *William Shakespeare's Get Thee Back to the Future*.

- **Five acts.** Plays in Shakespeare's time were structured in five parts, drawing on the tradition of ancient Roman plays. Acts can contain any number of scenes.
- **Minimal stage directions.** Shakespeare left it to the performers to determine who should do what on stage. I tried to do the same when writing *William Shakespeare's Get Thee Back to the Future*, but this play has far more stage directions than one of Shakespeare's would, to ensure that action sequences are clear. Shakespeare never had his characters try to jump-start a time-traveling automobile by wiring it to a clock tower in a thunderstorm, after all.
- **Rhyming couplets at the end of scenes.** A rhyming couplet is a pair of consecutive lines ending with a similar sound. For example, Act I, scene 3, lines 153–154 (see page 31): "'Tis strong and sudden, sent by heav'n above, / It may just save thy life, this pow'r of love." Shakespeare ended his scenes this way to indicate a narrative shift to the audience, similar to a final cadence in music.
- **Asides.** An aside is dialogue that the audience can hear but that the characters other than the speaker do not. These speeches often explain a character's motivations or inner thoughts or reveal

background information to the audience. We might also describe this as a character "breaking the fourth wall," that is, crossing the imaginary divide between stage and audience to address the spectators directly.

- **Soliloquies.** These monologues are similar to asides in that often they explain a character's behavior or motivation. But they occur when the character is alone on stage and tend to be longer than asides.

- **Anaphora.** Anaphora is the repetition of a word or phrase at the start of successive lines, used for rhetorical effect. See Doc's speech in Act I, scene 4, lines 236–240 (see page 50), in which he starts several lines with "A picture." (A similar speech appears in Shakespeare's *Henry the Sixth, Part 1*, Act II, scene 4, lines 11–15.)

DOC   A picture I would earnestly pursue,

A picture I would chase for thirty years,

A picture that was worth a thousand words,

A picture that gave unto me my aim,

My lifelong work: the flux capacitor.   240

- **Extended metaphors.** Shakespeare often draws out a metaphor in order to squeeze as much life from it as possible. One example is when Romeo and Juliet first meet and kiss in Act I, scene 5, of *Romeo and Juliet*; they make references to religion as an extended religious metaphor for their divine, nearly sacred love. Similarly, I used music as a metaphor in Act I, scene 2, lines 47–58 (see pages 26–27), in a conversation between Jennifer and Marty.

MARTY   When shall I ever have a chance to play

Before an audience with will to hear?

JENNIFER	Yet one rejection endeth not the world,	
	Nor doth it close the door on all thy dreams.	50
MARTY	Belike musician shall not be my trade,	
	For with an audience I strike no chords.	
JENNIFER	And yet thy talent sings in ev'ry note.	
	The record thou hast made of thy sweet songs,	
	With which thou wilt audition once again,	55
	Doth move me with its splendid melodies.	
	Send it, I bid thee, to a music shoppe	
	That will appreciate thine aptitude.	

- **Songs.** Shakespeare's plays are full of songs! Sometimes playful, sometimes mystical, sometimes sorrowful, songs appear at unexpected moments and often break the rhythm of iambic pentameter. *William Shakespeare's Get Thee Back to the Future* includes multiple songs adapted from the film's famous soundtrack, especially "The Power of Love" by Huey Lewis and the News (see page 30).

MARTY	[*sings:*] The pow'r of love, O 'tis a curious thing:
	It changeth hawks into a gentle dove,
	It maketh one man weep, another sing,
	More than a feeling: 'tis the pow'r of love.

SONNET 1.21

Get Thee Back to the Internet . . .

Doc, Marty, and his Jennifer set sail,
Toward an unknown, futuristic time.
We brave globetrotters, though, here end our tale—
No more of act and scene, of verse and rhyme.
Be not dismay'd—there's reason to rejoice!
Unto the **Quirk Books website** swiftly lead:
Discover further tales in Shakespeare's voice,
Which after this book thou mayst gladly read!
And other types of tomes await there too,
All sorts of wondrous volumes there abide.
Wouldst read an **Ian Doescher interview**?
Upon our pages such shall be supplied.
Hie thee unto the website in a trice.
Thou need'st not roads—just use thy smart device.

quirkbooks.com/gettheebacktothefuture